Also by Nora Raleigh Baskin

Anything But Typical,
Winner of the ALA Schneider Family Book Award

The Summer Before Boys

The Truth About My Bat Mitzvah

NORA RALEIGH BASKIN

Simon & Schuster Books for Young Readers
New York London Toronto Sydney New Delhi

SIMON & SCHUSTER BOOKS FOR YOUNG READERS
An imprint of Simon & Schuster Children's Publishing Division
1230 Avenue of the Americas, New York, New York 10020

For information about special discounts for bulk purchases,
please contact Simon & Schuster Special Sales at 1-866-506-1949
or business@simonandschuster.com.
The Simon & Schuster Speakers Bureau can bring authors to your live event.
For more information or to book an event,
contact the Simon & Schuster Speakers Bureau at 1-866-248-3049
or visit our website at www.simonspeakers.com.
Book design by Laurent Linn and Hilary Zarycky
The text for this book is set in Minister.
Manufactured in the United States of America • 0613 FFG
2 4 6 8 10 9 7 5 3 1
Library of Congress Cataloging-in-Publication Data
Baskin, Nora Raleigh.
Runt / Nora Raleigh Baskin.—First edition.
pages cm
Summary: From different perspectives, explores middle school bullying as Maggie,
tired of Elizabeth Moon's superior attitude, creates a fake profile on a popular social
networking site to teach Elizabeth a lesson.
ISBN 978-1-4424-5807-9 (hardback)
ISBN 978-1-4424-5809-3 (eBook)
[1. Bullying—Fiction. 2. Middle schools—Fiction. 3. Schools—Fiction. 4. Popularity—
Fiction. 5. Dogs—Fiction. 6. Online social networks—Fiction.] I. Title.
PZ7.B29233Run 2013
[Fic]—dc23
2012049461

FIRST
EDITION

For
Kelly, Maxine, Blanche, Willie, Sadie,
Eli (Manning Baskin),
and Kitty (née Goat)

And with all my heart I thank:

My editor, Alexandra Cooper, because writing is an individual art, and then it is not; I am so lucky to have someone who honors and respects both.

My agents, Marietta Zacker and Nancy Gallt, who need to remind me (quite often) that I do not have to be alone in this endeavor.

My children's-writers-who-breakfast friends, Elise Broach and Tony Abbott, who like to meet, have breakfast, and talk about the writing life.

My young friend, Jennifer Pagnoni, who wrote out my dialogue in text-message form, which was work for her and a complete leap of faith for me.

My son Sam, whose life experiences—because I feel them so deeply—he allows me to steal. I only hope I do them justice.

And for my son Ben, who is not only the author and voice of Matthew as well as the basketball team chorus, but talked to me whenever I demanded it about plot, theme, pacing, words, parents, pets, and life in middle school.

Any errors and near misses I claim as my own; for the good stuff I acknowledge the generosity of these insightful people.

"Outside of a dog,
a book is a man's best friend.
Inside of a dog,
it's too dark to read."

—*Groucho Marx*

THE ANSWERING VOICE

My mother says male dogs will fight. They will rise up on their hind legs and go for each other's necks. They will bare their teeth, snarl and bite, until one or the other gives up and then it's all over. And we can keep those two dogs right in the same room for the whole rest of their stay with us. As long as one is submissive, there won't be any more trouble, except for maybe a growl or two around their dinner bowls. Once boy dogs know the pecking order, it's all peaceful.

But girl dogs, my mother says, will fight to the death.

If we get an alpha female dog here, she'll go after the others and she won't give up, even when the other girl dog shows submission. If any dog got hurt while we were watching them, that would be the end of our business. But we agreed to take Sadie before we knew what she was like.

I don't always think my mother is right about the dogs. But after what happened with Sadie, my mom said she had a sneaking feeling all along. Sadie is a Saint Bernard so she's big, really big, and dogs know how big they are, believe me. It's like she knows just how much she weighs, which is about one hundred and seventy pounds. When I first met her, she leaned on me.

"That's just what she does," the owner said. "She's saying hello. But she can't talk."

Like I didn't know that.

"It's her way of hugging you," the owner went on.

I could tell they were anxious to get out of there. They were going to Club Med or Paradise Island or Disney World or something like that. They had a limo to catch to take them to the airport. I was just guessing that, but most everyone who brings their dog here is going somewhere.

But Sadie was not hugging me, that should have been the first clue. She was showing me who's boss and she thinks it's her. When the owner lady was not looking, I shoved Sadie back.

I bent down and looked her in the eye. "Not in my house," I whispered.

THE FISHER-REES BIRTHDAY PARTY

Miss Robinson was a bit chubby—okay, she was heavy—so when she wrote on the whiteboard, the flesh under her arm jiggled back and forth and some of the other kids giggled. *It's a good idea to giggle when others are giggling,* Maggie thought, *even if you don't know why.*

T-R-E-A-C-H-E-R-O-U-S, Miss Robinson wrote in red dry-erase.

The class often played this game at the end of the day when there were a few minutes left before the bell and Miss Robinson had already finished her lesson plan. It wasn't supposed to be a race, but the boys got all geared up and some of the girls, too. The object was to make as many words as you could using the letters in— for instance—treacherous. Then everyone shared their answers out loud, while Miss Robinson wrote the words on the board.

The students crossed off each word on their own list that was the same until someone had a word that no one else had. That person got a special prize from a drawer in Miss Robinson's desk, a new pencil or a ruler or a little spiral notepad. Maggie was used to winning things. She was smart and popular. She was pretty. But there was something about the time limit that she didn't like. Something about the big clock over the door ticking away the seconds and then minutes rendered all those things useless and left her confused.

Maggie felt her heart start to pound before Miss Robinson had even finished writing the word and she wanted her mind to start silently finding words but all she got was more nervous.

tree

her

a

at

Those were the easy words, the little ones. The kids that won always had some big long word that no one else thought of. Maybe a better tactic was to bypass the little words—everyone was going to get those anyway—and just concentrate on the big words.

teach

reach

In the five weeks they'd been in sixth grade, and every time they played this game using the week's vocab words, Maggie had never come close to winning and that's because everyone else was cheating.

They were not supposed to start until the word was completely written on the board and Miss Robinson said *Okay, begin,* but the boys were scribbling on whatever paper was already in front of them. Alex Pachman was using his permission slip for next week's field trip. Most of the girls had slipped a piece of paper out of their desk and started, except Elizabeth Moon, who is so weird anyway. She was just sitting there being obedient.

"Before we begin," Miss Robinson says, "can anyone tell me what this word means?"

Why are teachers so stupid they can't see what's going on? It's not fair. It's so unfair. By the time someone answered her, Maggie knew some kids would have ten or twelve or fifteen words down.

search

house

"Okay, now take out a clean sheet of paper and let's get started," Miss Robinson said. She went back to her desk and fiddled with something and didn't look up again.

It was so not fair.

Joey whatever-his-last-name-is won. After the words everyone had in common were crossed off, he had the last one and, wouldn't you know it, it was the easiest word.

Star.

He got to pick from the prize drawer, a plastic key chain with a Batman emblem.

Just before the end of the day, Miss Robinson called out, "Remember, tomorrow we start our unit on poetry. Everyone come in tomorrow with their favorite poem to share with the class."

"What if you don't have a favorite poem?" someone asked.

Good question.

"Ask your parents," Miss Robinson said. "They must have one. It's worth five points." Nobody was listening anymore. It was too close to the end of the day. People's brains started to shut down, but not Miss Robinson's.

"Hopefully we will put all your original poems

together and get it published for you to bring home and share with your parents. We will need someone to design our cover, and we can have a contest to pick just the right title. The class can vote for their favorite cover design and title."

If she said anything else it was drowned out by the final bell, the screeching metal chairs, and the stomping parade of sneakers out the door and onto the school buses.

Maggie's parents weren't home. Her mom was at work and her dad was in DC for a week. Five points toward her grade that she wouldn't be getting. So what else was new?

Angelica put out a snack, Goldfish and apple juice, and then began emptying the dishwasher. "Make sure to do all your homework before your mother gets home." Maggie liked Veronica better. Angelica was old and didn't want to play or even watch TV shows.

"I don't have any," Maggie answered.

"Suit yourself."

Maggie turned her computer on.

She needed to find a poem.

She could hear Angelica flitting around the other bedrooms, putting away clean clothes and mumbling to herself. Maggie kept her cell phone on vibrate, plugged in and charging, on the bed, her laptop propped up on her knees. Her television was on low—a *Degrassi* re-run—she wasn't supposed to watch TV until her homework was done. It was an episode she hadn't seen.

"I hope you are doing your schoolwork," Angelica's voice came up the stairs.

"*Home*work."

"Homework."

"I am," Maggie called back.

Maggie opened a blank document to begin her humanities paper on global conflicts. She picked the font and the line spacing and then clicked onto person2person to check for any after-school activity. She poked around a few people's pages. Zoe had changed her profile photo. Ethan posted a video. Maggie opened Google and typed in "World War II." She checked her cell phone for messages, went back to her person2person page, changed the channel on the TV, and then searched on Wikipedia for a while: horse racing, rugby (what's that?), soccer. Romans, the black death, stately homes. Then she typed one sentence:

Ireland is an island divided between <u>Republic of Ireland</u> (she copied and pasted) and part of the United Kingdom.

Enough homework for now. Maggie maximized her person2person profile. Gabby Fisher-Rees posted a photo from her fourth grade birthday party and five people had already commented. Maggie hadn't thought about Gabby in so long. Gabby had moved away, but every now and then she posted something and tagged someone from school.

Ethan—dang, I was good looking even back then

Stewart—Maybe on your planet, Ethan

Zoe—Don't listen to him, Ethan.

Larissa—OMG, look at my hair.

Stewart—nobody's looking. nobody cares, Larissa.

Gabby—thought you'd all like this blast from the past

Stewart—Matthew wasn't invited. Even in third grade Gabby had some taste.

Matthew—I didn't live here then, genius.

Stewart—poor excuse, Madeleine.

Zoe—Check it out Freida Goldstein wearing something other than all black.

The whole class had been invited to that party—the last year anybody did that. By fifth grade kids started inviting only friends and wannabe friends and leaving the used-to-be and never-really-were friends out. Maggie pushed her knees up to look more closely at the screen. Freida was wearing a pink T-shirt, or at least it looked pink in the tiny photo. Her purple sneakers with bright green shoelaces were poking out between all the other feet. She was original right from the start. She liked sticking out. She was already drawing really well by then, and making her own homemade jewelry.

But what was really different about Freida was that she was smiling and holding hands with her best friend. They were inseparable then. Smiling and holding hands and looking into the camera, Maggie and Freida. Freida and Maggie. People called them The Twins. Fourth grade was a long time ago.

EYES AND TEETH

Humanities

period 3

Freida Goldstein

In ancient Babylonian times the law was written on
a giant stone tablet. It mostly had to do with work
stuff, contracts, wages, liability. Some of it was about
family issues, divorce, marriage, money, children,
inheritance.

But naturally, the same rules didn't apply to
everyone.

Rich people, officials, kings and those people didn't
really have to follow the same procedures. But, given

the circumstances and the times, for most people it was better than nothing.

Another part of the tablet was about crimes that occurred. It was about punishment, about justice, about revenge. The Babylonians wanted to make sure that the retaliation a victim pursued was equal to the crime. No more. No less. Surely there had to be rules for taking someone's eye out.

These were not primitive peoples, after all. This was 1775 B.C.E., the height of culture and civilization. If a person caused another person's death, they should be put to death.

Fair's fair, as long as both parties belonged to the same social class.

A citizen was certainly allowed to try and seek justice outside his or her stratum. He or she could wait weeks, perhaps months, pay the appropriate court fees, and appear before the tribunal. The offended party of the lower class was then welcome to plead their case, present evidence, and ask for justice, but fat chances, bub.

There is the well-known story of the Babylonian sheep herder and the Hittite Princess, but its ending is far too gruesome to relate in this paper.

Of course, there is the famous yearlong trial of Ramses' two sons, both of whom believed he should be Pharaoh, but only one lived long enough to kill his father and take the throne.

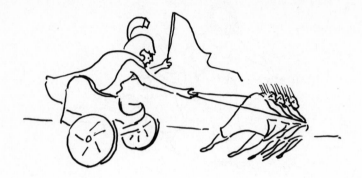

And how can anyone forget the case against Osiris, captain of the chariot team? Osiris was known to have lost over two hundred slaves due to his harsh and inhumane treatment, and was sued by his own stockholders.

The Ten Commandments (also written in stone, interestingly enough) came along about two hundred years after the Babylonian Code, and were a slightly improved version.

The Bible says, *Ayin tachat ayin.*

An eye for an eye.

But at least this time, the same rules were supposed to govern both the rich and the poor, both kings and peasants.

The Romans followed, with monetary compensation taking the place of an actual tooth or eye extraction.

And in modern times, of course, there are all sorts of safe and creative punishments for people who try to step out of their ascribed social standing.

No one, however—not Moses, not Hammurabi— could have predicted middle school.

B minus.
Very creative, Freida.
Great illustrations,
but you did not do the assignment.

THE MILLENNIAL GENERATION

Allison Robinson stared at herself in the mirror and made a pact with the higher powers, and at that moment she didn't really care which higher power was available. The mirror hung inside her closet door, and the door swung only partially open because the edge of Allison's desk stuck out too far. So in order to see her whole twelve-year-old body, Allison needed to stand partially inside the closet, pressed up against the shirts, skirts, dresses, and coats that never looked as good on, as they had in the store.

"Okay, so what's worse?" Allison asked aloud to herself. "Braces or being fat?" Allison wanted to be a teacher one day and she often practiced the art of directing a conversation with leading questions.

When no answer came she added another variable. "Or having pimples?"

In this case, Allison thought, logic could prevail. Braces weren't really part of your own body, so no one could really judge on how you looked with a mouthful of metal, right? But they certainly didn't help and they made your lips look puffy, so in that way braces were pretty ugly. Besides, if you were pretty to begin with and had straight teeth, you wouldn't need them.

Well, pimples aren't really your fault either, are they?

Allison's skin was clear, "like peaches and cream," her grandmother said. Allison's hair was dark with soft curls, the kind you only see in shampoo ads. And she had the longest, thickest lashes in the world, apparently, because whenever someone was trying to be nice, that's what they said. And apparently long, thick lashes were desirable, at least to old ladies and other plain, overweight girls.

So it's being fat. That's the worst.

"You're the farthest thing from fat," her dad said.

"I had the same exact body when I was your age. It's just baby fat," her mother said, and so Allison had scoured her mother's old childhood albums. The woman must have been delusional—Allison's mom looked like she weighed no more than sixty-five pounds when she was in sixth grade, with arms you could wrap your fingers around and legs so skinny there was no difference between the top thigh and calf.

And this was Allison's pact:

If I could be skinny I'll never ask for anything ever again.

Henry and Allison sat together at the far end of the cafeteria table, the table designated for those with nowhere else to sit. In her mind, Allison had dubbed it the No-Tolerance table.

"Do you know how many words you can spell with the letters in 'tolerance'?" Allison asked Henry.

"Where did that come from?"

"I don't know. Nowhere."

Allison liked Henry and not just because they had the same last name. He was smart and funny and shared things with her. He wasn't afraid to tell her embarrassing stories about his life. It made her feel like she could trust him and tell him things about herself, but Allison wouldn't dare tell him how she felt about him. Even Henry Robinson wouldn't want to hook up with a girl like her.

If I could be skinny I'll never ask for anything ever again.

"There's nothing worse than being unpopular in sixth grade," Allison said.

"Now where did *that* come from?"

Allison shrugged.

Henry said, "But since you asked, I will tell you what's worse than being unpopular in sixth grade, which, by the way, you are not. Popularity is all relative."

She knew it wasn't true, but it felt good all the same.

"Being stupid," Henry told Allison. "That would be worse. Being dumb is the kiss of death."

"You're probably right. And by the way, it's fifty-seven."

"What is? The number of words in 'tolerance'?"

Allison nodded. Henry was smart. And he had really pretty blue eyes.

Henry balled up the wrapper from his sandwich and stuffed it back into his bag. "That's it? Fifty-seven?"

"Yup." Allison really had no idea how many words you could make with the letters in the word tolerance but she made a mental note to go home and try it out.

"Is lunch almost over?" Henry asked.

The rest of their class seemed to be done eating and were engaging in various other activities—passing notes, emptying out the contents of Pixy Stix onto the table, carving their initials in the formica.

"Hey, Allison."

Henry and Allison both looked up. It was never good to be noticed during lunch—or any other time for that matter, but particularly during lunch.

"Hey, Allison. Smile."

There was some laughter coming from somewhere.

"C'mon, smile."

Allison didn't, but one of the girls, surrounded by other girls, at the far end of the table, snapped a picture with a tiny camera. It was Cynthia Conrad.

"It's my new sticky-film Polaroid. It's so super cool," Cynthia Conrad announced, though no one had asked her. "Just hope you didn't break the lens." That line seemed to elicit a round of wild giggles.

"No good will come of that," Henry whispered.

"It's just a picture. It can't hurt me," Allison said. She picked up her lunch tray. "C'mon. Let's go outside."

"Don't worry. She'll get hers."

Allison dumped her trash into the garbage and dropped her tray on the conveyor belt that fed the dirty dishes back into the kitchen.

"What do you mean?"

"Everybody gets theirs, one way or another. One day or another. I have proof."

Allison laughed. "I wish I believed that. I wish I knew that one day someone would be really mean to Cynthia Conrad and she'd feel bad about how she treats other people."

"I didn't say anyone was going to feel bad. I just said they'll get theirs."

"Okay, so what's your proof?" They walked outside. It was freezing.

Henry spread his arms out wide. "Right there," he said.

Allison looked at the trees and let her eyes scan the playground. Most everyone was standing around with their arms wrapped around their bodies, trying to keep warm. A few boys were kicking a ball around on the grass.

"Where?"

"No, out there. Look past the playground and softball field. Look—there is life after middle school."

Allison laughed.

"Besides, in another year nobody's going to want a

Polaroid. Cynthia will be using her super cool new camera as a paperweight. Within ten years everything's going to be digital."

"Digital?" Allison asked. "What's that?"

THE ANSWERING VOICE II

My pant leg is covered with dog hair. I notice it as soon as I get to class. But what else is new?

"You smell, Elizabeth," Justin Benton says to me. Justin always tells me I smell.

"So do you." I sit down at my desk right behind his. He doesn't smell, though, and I probably do. I probably do, but I'm so used to it I can't even tell anymore. It's in our clothes—anything made of natural fabric—jeans, sweatshirts. And hair. Hair really holds on to smells. I should just wear polyester and shave my head.

Bet I'd be real popular then.

"You stink like dog pee," Justin stands up and leans over into my space just to say this. I swipe at him, but before I can knuckle him in the arm, he drops back down into his seat.

"Dummy," I say. It's all I can think of.

Anyway, he is a dummy because it isn't pee. There's no pee on me. It's just the smell of all the animals in our house; all the dogs that come and go. All of them are housebroken. So it's not pee.

"Miss Robinson?" Hannah Montana raises her hand. Well, that's just what I call her. She's so stuck-up and she's skinny like Miley Cyrus with a round face like hers.

"Maggie?" Miss Robinson calls on her and I already know what she's going to ask.

"Can I move my seat?" This question is followed by a very low rumble of giggles, like a tiny wave set into motion by a bug scooting across a pond.

Miss Robinson looks up from where she's sitting behind her desk, presumably to assess the situation. *Now, why would this girl want to move her seat?* We have all just put our heads down to start this vocabulary test. It's real quiet in the room (or at least it was) and for no apparent reason, out of the blue, Hannah Montana needs to change her seat.

"Not now, Maggie," Miss Robinson says. She gives

her an austere (that is one of our vocabulary words this week) look and Maggie knows that I know that Miss Robinson knows exactly why she wants to move away from me. Maggie wants everyone to laugh.

"Now get back to your papers, everyone. Seventeen minutes left." She says that, but Miss Robinson has never taken a test away from anyone who was still working. She's nice like that. She's kind of big and round but she's got the prettiest face and the nicest smile. She always asks me about Mork and Mindy, and about Lola because she took one of our kittens last year, before she got this job teaching sixth grade and she was still a student teacher in the elementary school.

I am not the last one finished with my test, but close. I am pretty sure I aced it, as vocabulary is my forte.

All things considered and not considering Justin Benton or Hannah Montana, it's an okay day, actually. Miss Robinson hands out our newly printed creative writing anthologies. It's all our work from the last month, from our unit on poetry. They were all printed out and stapled together. Larissa Joyce got to do the cover. Everyone got to pick a name we wanted for our anthology then Miss Robinson put them on the board and we voted. I didn't win. Mine was *Write On!* but I don't think anyone got the play on words or else it might have won.

Ethan won instead, so our class poetry anthology is called *The Answering Voice*. When I hold it in my hands I see how shiny the cover is and how heavy and beautiful the book is. The first thing I want to do is flip to my own poem, but I wait until I get home. I don't even open it up.

I wait the whole bus ride. It's like lying in bed Christmas morning waiting for the sun to come up.

Sadie is hunting, my mother tells me. We've got to keep her away from Mrs. Smallman's bichons.

Mrs. Smallman had left her three bichon frises for two weeks while she is on a cruise with Mr. Smallman. They are regulars and those three dogs know their way around our house. They even got in the car with my mom and me when we went out. In general they stuck close together. They are all girls, Winkie, Blinkie, and Nod, though I sure couldn't tell them apart.

"Where is she?"

"Sadie?" My mother looks up from the TV.

"What are you doing? Find her, Elizabeth. Hurry."

You'd think nobody would be able to lose a hundred-and-seventy-pound dog, but it takes me a while to find her. She is laying on the floor in the hall right outside the laundry room, blocking the whole exit, and sure enough Winkie, or Blinkie, or Nod is hiding behind the washer.

"Outta here, Sadie," I shout. I give her a little nudge with my foot but she doesn't move. I say it louder and with a deeper voice. From experience, I've figured out that stubborn dogs will respond more to male voices. I think in general, the dads in their families are more alpha than the moms, so basically I am trying to sound like a dad.

"Move it, Sadie!"

Finally she struggles to her feet—her front legs, paws first, and then she lifts her whole back end. But she just stands there.

"Let's go, girl," I say and she follows me into the kitchen. Dogs will always follow you into the kitchen. They know that's where food comes from.

We've never had a Saint Bernard here but I'm learning fast. They drool into their water bowls (at least Sadie does) a ton, *every* time they take a drink, so I have to bend down and change it every time. It's like she's just making sure any dog who tries to take a drink after her has to go thirsty or drink her spit. We have five water bowls lined up and it looks like she's spit in four of them.

Then I remember *The Answering Voice*. I haven't shown my mother yet. I pull it out of my backpack, but first I sit down on the floor and run my hands over the cover. It's in color and kind of bumpy like a real book. Larissa did a good job. She even made the title look like part of the picture, all swirly, but you can still read it.

There is a table of contents.

My poem is on page eleven.

The page numbers are on the bottom right.

There it is.

Reincarnation

It's short, only three lines:

Rain keeps me from school
So I stayed home with the dogs
I grew large white fangs

It's a haiku which is five, seven, five. Five syllables in the first line, then seven, and then five syllables in the last line. But nobody is going to know that. I love the way it looks on the page, all white around it. The letters dark and simple.

I flip around to some of the other poems, mostly about summer and sunshine or someone's favorite vacation. Or about all of the above. A lot of the poems rhyme, like Jessie Peterson's:

I love summer and summer loves me.
The sun shines all day, even underneath the trees

We love to go on vacation and sit at the beach all day
Where there is nothing else to do but play, and play and
play.

I love summer and summer loves me.
It's best season of all with so much to do and see.

That's pretty bad but you know no one is going to tell her that. I'm sure not. She's not my best friend. That's something you'd only tell your best friend, to help her out. I don't really have any one particular friend.

Very carefully I close the anthology and stand up— or I am about to stand up—and show it to my mom. I notice Sadie is not standing next to me anymore but I don't think anything of that until I hear my mother yelling, really yelling.

To break up a dogfight you have to be really confident. You have to be unafraid to kick one of the dogs in the side, shout really loud, and let them both know you are in charge. Use a broom handle, anything. And my mother has always told me never to break up a dogfight. Never get in the mix. By the time I run into the den it's over and there is blood all over the floor.

"It's Nod," my mother says. "We've got to get her to the vet."

Sadie is sitting in the corner with guilt written all over her face.

"And get the big cage out from the basement, Elizabeth."

I feel bad for Sadie. She didn't mean it. For all she knows she's here for good. For all she knows her mom and dad left her forever and this is where she's got to stay, so she's just trying to find her place.

"Elizabeth, quick."

By the time we get back, it's late and dark. My mother makes Sadie sleep in that crate all night. I can hear her whimpering from my bedroom. I try to shut my door but it almost sounds louder.

"It's okay, Sadie. I know you didn't mean it." I am kneeling next to her. She barely fits in there. I know she can't turn around. Maybe she's thirsty, so I bring her some water in a plastic dish, but she can't get her snout out between the bars to drink. If I open the door, even just a little, she'll push her way out and I'll never get her back in.

It turned out to be Blinkie, not Nod, that got into the fight. Now she has a big bite in her tongue. Lots of blood, the vet told us, but nothing we can do but let it heal. He gave us some antibiotics. My mother prayed all the way home that Mrs. Smallman doesn't notice. The bleeding stopped and you can only see the wound when Blinkie opens up her mouth.

Thank the Lord dogs can't talk, my mother says.

"It's okay, Sadie," I say. "Your mommy and daddy are coming back soon. And then you'll be out of there."

Sadie cries, little breathing cries, all night.

It isn't until just before I fall back asleep, right there on the rug in the den, that I remember *The Answering Voice*. I never got to show my mom.

Tomorrow.

WHAT DOESN'T KILL YOU

For five hundred years, the horses have run free on the outer banks of North Carolina. Since he was a baby, Ethan and his family have been renting a house with the Zingone family, on the beach in Corolla. Ethan's father and Don Zingone had gone to college together in Virginia, and even though the two families both lived states away, they'd spent this week together on the outer banks for the last ten years. But never once, in all those boiling hot summer days, had Ethan seen a wild horse.

"If the hurricane comes this way we'll have to evacuate." Jamie Zingone shook the Boggle cube.

"No, we won't," Jamie's little brother, Benjamin, said.

"Oh, yes we will, and we might have to leave you

behind," Jamie answered his brother.

Ethan lay with his feet stretched out over the arm of the couch, his head resting on the other end. He was staring up, watching the huge paddles of the ceiling fan turning slowly. Hanging clumps of dark dust threatened to fly off at any moment and land right on Jamie's head. That's the kind of summer it was.

Benjamin asked again. "That would never happen, would it, Ethan?"

Benjamin was seven. Ethan ten. Jamie Zingone was a year and a half older than that. The last thing Ethan needed was to have Jamie's little brother thinking he had an ally in Ethan. It wouldn't help Ethan's status with Jamie at all.

"How do I know?" Ethan answered.

He didn't know, and to tell the truth he was a little scared about the darkening sky and the weather reports. After a full day at the beach, the parents were all up on the main floor where the kitchen was. The kids mostly stayed downstairs where the television was. Ethan felt bad for Benjamin, but what could he do?

Yesterday Jamie and Benjamin's mom made a run to the supermarket for groceries, and for some reason—

maybe to have some influence over the selection of ice cream and cookies—all three boys went along. All three sat in the backseat; Jamie had one window seat, Ethan the other, and Benjamin, being the youngest, was stuck in the middle. At some point during the drive, Jamie gave Ethan the signal to push Benjamin as hard as he could.

"Squeeze him," Jamie ordered. He dug his shoulder and hip into his little brother. Ethan did the same, until Benjamin's eyes sprung with tears. Until Jamie and Benjamin's mother told them to stop. She glared at Ethan in particular, as if this behavior was more expected from an older brother.

But wasn't it obvious? If Ethan hadn't joined in, next time Jamie would do it to him.

Go along to get along, right?

What choice did he have?

But it all seemed to be forgotten at the beach today, even if Jamie was being especially mean to his brother right now, picking on his fear of the storm.

"Well, I'm going to tell Mom." Benjamin put down his Boggle pad and stood up. "And you're going to get in trouble."

He did everything a kid brother should never do. He

was literally asking for it, and he kept coming back for more. Jamie imitated his voice and told him to go ahead and tell his mommy how scared he was. Benjamin ran up the stairs.

"You wanna play?" Jamie asked Ethan. He shook the Boggle cube again and started writing down his words. The weird thing was that when his little brother wasn't around, Jamie was really pretty nice.

"Sure." Ethan rolled off the couch and sat cross-legged across from Jamie, just as a flash of lightning brightened the room, followed a few moments later by a loud clap of thunder and an immediate downpour of rain.

"Wow, that is coming closer." Jamie stood up. The rain was deafening.

Both boys ran up the stairs. It was four in the afternoon and the sky was completely dark. No one upstairs seemed worried.

"Remember the summer it rained the whole week?" Jamie's mom was saying.

Ethan's mom had a book in her lap but she wasn't reading. "Yeah, until the very last day the sun came out, and we had to pack up and leave." She looked over at Ethan. "You were just a baby. And Benjamin wasn't even born yet."

"But I was a year later!" Benjamin shouted.

"What a genius," Jamie felt compelled to add.

It always surprised Ethan that Jamie's parents never said anything about the nasty comments and jokes Jamie made about his little brother.

The two dads were standing in the kitchen, leaning on the counter watching the rain through the wide sliding glass doors. "We'll have to ride this one out too."

"No fishing."

"Nope."

"Too early for a beer?"

Jamie's mom answered her husband. "Yes, too early."

Another flash of light and the boys all started counting.

"Three one thousand." Benjamin threw his hands up into the air. "It's three miles away."

"Oh goody, Benjamin learned to count in nursery school this year." For that remark, his mother gave Jamie a look, but that was the extent of it. It made Ethan glad he didn't have an older brother.

The two families made spaghetti and salad that night, watched a movie on pay-per-view, and then got ready for bed. The three boys slept in the same room, two sets of bunk beds. Jamie on top and Benjamin on the bottom. Ethan had chosen the bottom bunk as well by claiming the mattress was more comfortable.

"Mommy," Benjamin called out. The lights in the room were already turned off. Only a straight beam of white cut across the floor from the light in the hall bathroom. "Come and tuck me in."

"You're such a baby." Jamie leaned over his bunk and swatted at his brother.

Their mother came in. Ethan could hear the bed creak as she sat down on the edge of Benjamin's bed and pulled the covers up to his shoulders. They were in shadows but Ethan could hear every word.

"Mom?" Benjamin whispered.

"Mm-hmm."

"What happens to the horses?" The rain was steadily pelting the windows. Every so often the wind would pick up and it was like someone had thrown a bucket of water at the house.

"What horses, sweetie?"

"The wild horses. The ones that live on the beach. The ones that swam ashore when the Spanish boat sank in 1587."

Where did Benjamin learn all that? Ethan opened his eyes wide to take in any light and turned his head away from his pillow to hear better.

"They'll be fine, Benjamin," his mother said.

How does she know? Ethan thought.

"How do you know?" Benjamin asked his mother. "This is a *hurricane*. And they are an endangered species. There's only a hundred of them left. That sounds like a lot, but it's not."

Jeez.

"I'm sure they are used to this weather if they've been here for five hundred years."

"Not each horse. Each horse hasn't been here for five hundred years. Just the herd."

"Then they're pretty strong and they'll be fine."

"But how do you *know*?"

"It's survival of the fittest, sweetie. It's nature's way."

Ethan heard her kiss him. She said good night to the rest of them, the light from the bathroom momentarily cutting her body in two when she stood up, then she slipped out the door.

Ethan fell asleep thinking about the horses, as the rain pounded the house all night.

NOTHING LEFT TO LOSE

Freida knew Maggie wouldn't vote for her poetry anthology cover and that Maggie would somehow be able to get the whole class to vote for someone *she* wanted to have win. That someone would, of course, be Larissa Peterson.

She knew it, even as she sat at her dining room table at home and worked on her design. Lots of people can draw really well, Maggie thought. Even Larissa. The key to being an artist is to be different, do something in a new way, with an original voice. Like they were always saying on *American Idol*: *Make it your own.*

Freida had a drawer in the kitchen that held all her art supplies, scissors, tape, fimo clay, paper, glue, ribbons, glitter, paints and brushes, stapler, hole punch, rubber stamps, markers, colored pencils, charcoal pencils, gesso board, an X-Acto knife that her mother didn't know was there. And on the outside of the drawer she had taped a sign: DO NOT OPEN.

It was open now and all the found objects Freida had been collecting were spread out on the table. Something to represent everyone in the class. A blue feather for Elizabeth's blue eyes. Half of an old lace from a basketball sneaker for Matthew. The torn cover of a fashion magazine for Zoe.

She carefully took apart one of her dad's old watches and separated the tiniest metal pieces on the board to represent time, the time they had spent together, in light and in dark. She had the wrapper to Kyle's favorite candy bar, a piece of the Nigerian flag because Assumpta's mother had been an African princess. For Ethan she found an actual strip of used film since he was so into photography now.

Only for Maggie she drew. It took most of the evening. She drew what Aristophanes described as the first humans, combined as one powerful being that spun on four legs like a wheel. Then she carefully glued all the other pieces over it, so only if you looked very carefully could you see what lay underneath.

"Oh my goodness, that's incredible." Freida's mother walked into the dining room. "I wondered what you were doing in here so long."

Freida held it up. The name of the anthology—when the class chose it—would go right in the center. She left a space so that nothing would be completely covered, but nothing would stand out more than anything else.

"Freida, it's lovely. When you stand back"—her mother took a few steps back—"it just looks like one colorful piece, but up close you see all the details. Is it for a special project?"

Freida looked at the board, her design, the work she put into it. It would be too hard to duplicate anyway. They would have to photograph it at a high resolution and reproduce it in three, if not four, colors. It would be too expensive. And besides, Larissa would win. Maggie would make sure of that.

"No," Freida answered. "I just made it for me."

"It's great you have that freedom, Freida," her mother said. "I'm so proud of you."

Sometimes it was better to get out of the game altogether instead of worrying if you were winning or losing.

COINCIDENCE |kō'-in(t)-sə-den(t)s|

noun

1 a remarkable concurrence of events or circumstances without apparent causal connection : *it's no coincidence that this new burst of innovation has occurred in the free nations | they met* **by coincidence.**
2 correspondence in nature or in time of occurrence : *the coincidence of interest between the mining companies and certain politicians.*
3 Physics the presence of ionizing particles or other objects in two or more detectors simultaneously, or of two or more signals simultaneously in a circuit.

And the funny part was that she wasn't going to have to change her name.

Only Elizabeth didn't think there was anything funny

about any of it. Miss Robinson told the class she was getting married. She made it into one of her word games. Elizabeth didn't write down one word (even though *coincidence* was such an easy one). She just sat there wondering how she was going to get by for the two weeks Miss Robinson—who would henceforth be known as Mrs. Robinson—was away on her honeymoon.

coin

den

nice

need

Sometimes Elizabeth dreamed about Miss Robinson. She dreamed Miss Robinson was her mother and they went on picnics together. It must have been something she had seen in a TV commercial, with a red checkered blanket and a wicker basket, because on the picnic, in the dream, she spilled ketchup on her shirt and Miss Robinson cleaned it up right away with some special laundry detergent and she didn't get mad at all.

Miss Robinson never got mad. She taught language arts and social studies. She had her own library in the back of the room and kids were allowed to borrow books without signing them out or being told to be quiet while finding one. She called it the honor system. She expected you to return the book. If you lost it, she expected you to replace it with some other (appropriate) book, but she didn't get mad.

It's not that Elizabeth didn't love her own mother. She did.

It was just a dream.

ice

dice

no

in

Regina Rashad won this time. She got to pick her prize from the drawer. Then Miss Robinson told everyone to take out their notebooks. It was time for language arts.

"I'd like to ask everyone what their parents thought of our anthology."

"*The Answering Voice*," Ethan called out.

"*The Answering Voice*," Miss Robinson agreed. "So let's go around the room. I'd love to hear."

Even the desks in Miss Robinson's room were arranged in a special way, like a giant horseshoe, two horseshoes—one smaller one inside the bigger one, everyone facing the back of the room, where Miss Robinson sat directly in front of all her books. She started at the far left, outer horseshoe.

"My mom and dad loved it."

"Very creative and wonderful."

And then once somebody had used a word, it seemed it was the only word the next five people could remember.

"Just like a real book. The poems were all so creative."

"Really creative."

"All the poems were really creative."

"Wonderful and creative."

"My mom said it was really creative. She loved it."

Elizabeth counted the number of kids till Miss Robinson got to her and asked what her parents thought of *The Answering Voice*. Only her mother hadn't seen the book of poetry. Her mother didn't even know about it, and Elizabeth hadn't talked to her father in three years—which was actually a very good thing, according to Elizabeth's mom.

So what would Elizabeth say? She had had all weekend to show her mom. She had Friday night and all day Saturday and all day Sunday. Friday was the vet and then there was Saturday.

"Not now, Lizzybeth," her mother said. "Just let me

sleep a little bit." And somehow the day got away from them. Her mother got up by lunch. The dogs needed to be fed. The kitty litter changed. There were two rabbits now, still outside in their hutch. At night her mother had her favorite shows on TV.

And then Sunday, after church. They stopped at the A&P for one of those already-cooked chickens. To be fair, Elizabeth probably forgot about it for a while on Sunday and then by nightfall, who knows?

"Elizabeth?"

She loved Miss Robinson. Miss Robinson thought she was smart. She liked Elizabeth's writing, her stories. Elizabeth always got a hundred on the vocabulary quizzes. Her best skill was using the vocabulary word in a sentence. But not just any sentence, like Maggie did when the word was "anticipate."

"I like to anticipate the new year," Maggie said, and Miss Robinson said that was good.

Elizabeth raised her hand. "They failed to *anticipate* the rain and so everyone at the picnic got wet because they didn't bring umbrellas."

"Perfect, Elizabeth," Miss Robinson said. "That so perfectly illustrates the meaning of the word."

"Did your mother like the poetry book?" Miss Robinson was asking.

She didn't know how to answer, but Elizabeth started talking anyway, hoping maybe, she could find that feeling again, that so-good feeling she got when Miss Robinson was happy with her.

"My mother thought mine was better than everyone else's." And once she had begun she just kept going. "I mean, the others were cute, like about snow and sunshine and everything. But my mother said mine was different. It was more meaningful." There was no stopping her. "And my dad said mine was the best too. Rhyming poems are silly, he said. He liked mine the best because it didn't rhyme. And it was about something. Meaningful, you know?"

The whole room was suddenly very quiet and very very hot. Elizabeth knew there probably wasn't a laundry detergent in the whole world that could get this stain out.

MASS HYSTERIA

Zoe: Ugg.. I haaaate goin to the orthodontist

Maggie: no fun.. but mayb u will c sum cute boyz in the w8ting room ;)

Zoe: we r l8 as usual

Zoe: of course my mom is blabbin on her cell && speeding.. smaarrrt

Maggie: wut? she tlkng crap bout sumbody?

Zoe: ya.. shocking

Maggie: wuts she tlkng bout now?

Zoe: wellll.. I guess she saw Larissas mom wearin a fake Louis

Maggie: lame.. tell her 2 get a life

Zoe: so annoying.. she won't stop tlkng bout it >:o

Zoe: least shes not comin in w/ me

Zoe: Hello?

Zoe: u still thr?

Zoe: ugg! its packed in here.. gunna take 4ever! ☹

Maggie: read a magazine?

Zoe: no gud 1s they r all old ☹

Zoe: Oh snap.. qt alert!!!!

Maggie: o ya!?!

Zoe: ya just checkin out my competition haha

Maggie: lol u r funny.. lyke WE have competition

Maggie: soooo..nething gud??

Zoe: HAH! O man.. freckle-face miiiight have a chance lolol!

Zoe: Maggie u shud c this grl!! She prob has lyke 1002429834 freckles all over her skinny body.. yuck!

Maggie: pretty skinny or throw up skinny?

Zoe: Pretty skinny but UGLY jeans haha

Maggie: wut wud u rank her?

Zoe : hmm on a scale from 1 – 10…

Zoe: 5.5.. 2 below me n 3 below u lolol ☺

Maggie: k next!

Zoe: uh oh.. i c sum possible competition.

Zoe: Perf hair.. perf skin.. u kno 1 of those grls

Maggie: pretends she doesn't kno shes pretty type?

Zoe: ya exactly! Shes a little chubby tho.. bet she will get fat in high school haha

Maggie: lol ☺

Zoe: OMG! OMG! OMG!

Maggie: wut!?!

Zoe: major HOTTIE just wlkd in!!!

Maggie: How hott!?!

Zoe: outta 10?? ummm def 11!!

Maggie: ow! ow! go tlk 2 him grl!

Maggie: hello?

Maggie: r u tlkng 2 him!?!

Zoe: Im here n noooo I cant!

Maggie: wut? y not?

Zoe: b/cuz of this gigantic pimple taking over my face! ☹☹

Maggie: OMG grl stop! I bet u cant even c it!

Zoe: OMG Mag! Yes u can!! u r the 1 who pointed it out 2 me, member???

Maggie: Zoe I was jk!

Maggie: Now stop bein a big baby n go tlk 2 him!!! ☺

Zoe: Nope. Not happening. I luk like Natasha!! ☹

Maggie: who the heck is Natasha?

Zoe: u kno.. Freida's sister..wutshername?

Maggie: OOoh Nadine hahaha ya dum dum! ☺

Maggie: haha jk

Zoe: ya w/e Nadine Natasha..

Zoe: u kno how she tries 2 cover it all up w/ makeup but by the end of the day her face just looks lyke a melting pizza hahaha gross!

Maggie: hahaha ya def a cake face lol

Maggie: hey I g2g grl! Luvs u! xoxo

Zoe: kk my name just got called newayz

Zoe: t2ul grl ,<3 ya 2! xoxo

TRASH

I told my mom what Elizabeth Moon said in Lan-
guage Arts today and she said that trash is always trash.
She said money can't buy you class. And I said, But Elizabeth Moon doesn't have money, she's poor, her mom takes
dogs into their house for a job. And my mother said, Well
see, that's exactly what I mean, and she then told Angelica
to make me chicken nuggets for dinner and she went in to
her office to prepare for her conference call to China.

Except that it wasn't really what Elizabeth said about
her own poem being better than everyone else's that was
bothering me, it was what happened in the cafeteria right
afterward. And anyway, Stewart thought it was funny.
And Zoe. So did Ethan, and Matthew and everyone else

except for you, which you would have, if you had any sense of humor left. Anyway, we were just kidding.

"Miss Maggie?"

My bedroom door was shut. Remember when you used to sleep over all the time, like every weekend? And we would stay up and draw under the covers in our sketch pads with that huge flashlight? And we made up that name to call ourselves, "Magda", because "Freiggie" just didn't sound right.

"You food is ready."

See, even Angelica can't call it dinner.

"Did my dad call?" I shouted back at the door.

"Not yet, Miss Maggie. Now hurry and can come down to eat. The nuggens—"

"Nuggets."

"The *nuggets* are not good when they are cold."

They're not so good hot either, but I didn't say that. Instead I asked Angelica if I could eat in my room. She said that was okay, probably because that way she doesn't have to look at me and feel bad about herself for being just a housekeeper and having no life.

Seriously, nobody likes you the way you are now. You used to be a lot more fun.

Remember, Freida? Remember we were both walkers in fourth grade before middle school and remember how we got to swing on the swings when everybody had already left to catch their bus? And even with all those empty swings we both sat together in the same seat?

"We are like those human beings in social studies class," you said.

We pumped our legs up and stretched them up into the air until the toes of our sneakers were visible against the blue of the sky.

"Oh, yeah!" I shouted. "Before the head God-guy got mad and split them apart."

"Jealous," you told me. "He was jealous because the humans were so powerful."

"Zeus." I remembered his name. We were having a test on Greek mythology the next day.

"Humans had four legs and four arms and ran across the ground like a wheel faster than the gods could run."

We each held on to one side of the swing and wrapped our other arms around each other, leaning forward into the backswing and back against the rushing wind and up into the sky again.

"But we found each other," I said. "And now nothing can stop us."

"We are so powerful."

The dirt under the swing, where countless feet had run before us, was dug into a narrow groove, with tufts of grass on either side. The ground sped into a blur of green and brown the higher and faster we got. Four legs, four arms, four feet, four hands, two heads, two bellies, two laughing girls.

There was no one else in the world but us.

Just last week, my mom asked me why we weren't friends anymore and I had to tell her something, so I said it was because you had turned in a major traitor in middle school, which is kind of true if you think about it.

SCHOOL SPIRIT

I don't *like* like her that way, but Maggie is really pretty and she practically begged me to help her. She wanted me to take a picture of Elizabeth Moon. I can't imagine Maggie has honorable intentions, but like I said, she practically begged me. And she's really pretty.

The truth is I may even want to be a photographer one day.

This is already my second digital camera, but over the summer I took black and white photography at the Arts Center in town. It was completely different. You have no idea what your picture is going to look like until you get into the darkroom, and even then you can mess the whole thing up in the developing process. But when you are in the little room, in the dark, and an image starts to appear on this blank piece of paper in the chemicals, and you think, *Wow, that's a great shot*, it's really cool.

"You working on the paper, Ethan?"

We don't even have a school paper. You would think the assistant principal would know that.

"Uh, yes sir, I am," I said. I lowered my camera and waited until he walked away.

You can do some things to a photographic image in the darkroom with the light exposure and the enlarger but nothing like you can with a digital picture in Photoshop. In digital you can fix everything and anything. Change anything from color to shape to location. It hardly matters what you took a picture of in the first place. It's like you can turn anything into something else if you want to and you know how.

It's all perception.

"What are you up, to E-man?" It's Stewart. He's on the travel basketball team with me. He thinks he's better than everyone else too, but he probably is.

"Nothing," I said.

"Then what's with the camera?"

We were all headed into the field house to learn the

school song. The idea is by the time we get to high school everyone knows it, but that never happens. We had to walk outside to get to the field house and the trees were hung in maroon and gold, our school colors. The colors of the T-shirts we were all wearing too.

"I'm taking pictures, what does it look like?"

Stewart jumped in front of me and stopped dead. I nearly banged into him.

"Take one of me, E-man." he said.

"Fine. Do something interesting."

I clearly shouldn't have said that.

Hordes of kids were passing us on each side, a blur of maroon and yellow. It took Stewart no time at all to find his target since pretty much one out of every two kids that passed by was of some lower strata than he was, at least according to the hierarchy of middle school.

But right now, there seemed to be no life past getting rid of Stewart and getting Maggie the photo she wanted.

"Okay, whoa. How about this?" Stewart had grabbed one of the boys in the hall and urged him to the floor. "C'mon, Dexter, just get down on your hands and knees so I can stand on you."

"No way, Stewart," the boy answered. He pushed

back and seemed temporarily freed but unable to get by and continue on.

Stewart gave the boy another friendly push, this time in my direction. "It's for a picture, jerk-off. Just do it. You ready with your camera, E-man?"

The boy looked over and caught my eye. I didn't know his name but I knew it probably wasn't Dexter. It definitely wasn't *Jerk-off*. The boy was pretty big, taller than either me or Stewart, but not heavier. Stewart had no trouble holding him still.

"Whatcha waiting for, E-man?"

Stewart hopped up onto the boy's back, his arms outstretched, which gave me a fraction of a second to snap a wide angle, 33 mm, 15 aperture exposure. *The Decisive Moment.* That's what my photography teacher had taught us. It would be a great shot: victory on Stewart's face and the grimace of defeat on the boy's. Stewart would love it. Probably post it on person2person.

"Leave him alone," I said. "I gotta go." I tried to step aside.

And there was a long moment, long like a movie in slow motion. Stewart looked at the boy, and then back to me. The boy. Me.

He was angry.

"Then I'll take the picture," Stewart said, and he grabbed the camera out of my hand. "How about your face in a headlock? That's a funny one, right, Poindexter?"

It turns out Dexter did outweigh me by quite a bit. He stepped behind me and wrapped his arm around my shoulder and across my neck, causing me to bend over, but forcing my head upright and directly into the lens. Of my own camera.

"Sweet." Stewart held the camera to his face and pushed the shutter release.

I could still feel the pressure from Stewart's arm around my neck when I found Elizabeth Moon and snapped her photo. I didn't know what Maggie wanted with the photo, but right at that moment I didn't care anymore.

JUST KIDDING

My mother told Sadie's owners they couldn't bring her to us anymore. She told them when they came to the door to pick her up. The man and the woman, all suntanned. That's usually how their faces look when they come to get their dogs, all tan. Sometimes red and peeling in papery sheets of skin, and they pay big bucks for that look.

"But why?" the woman asked. The man was writing out a check so maybe he didn't hear at first.

"Because she's a bully," my mother said. "She's big. Bigger than the other dogs and she knows it."

I watched the look on the woman's face. Her eyes got all watery. I didn't know that happened to grown-ups.

"Sadie?" The woman couldn't believe it. She kept blinking, hard. "But she's so sweet."

"Well, sure." My mother wasn't one to pull any punches. "She's sweet to you, but in a group she's a bully. A first-rate bully."

"But I—"

"Don't take it personal. I just can't take her in here anymore."

Thank God my mother had taken down the crate and put it away before Sadie's owners showed up. I think that would have put this woman right over the edge—literally, maybe.

"What did she do, exactly?" The man handed my mother his check and then leaned down to clip the leash onto Sadie's collar. He stood and waited for an answer.

"Intimidation. She let the others know who was boss. It got to where the other dogs wouldn't eat from their own bowls unless I put Sadie away."

"Put her away?" It was the woman again.

"Outside," I answered. "She had to wait outside until the other dogs had eaten."

Everyone got quiet.

"I don't believe it," the man said finally. "You just

didn't let her know you were the boss. She didn't feel safe here. Someone needs to be the alpha dog."

"Well, then it's best for everyone, isn't it?" My mother opened the front door. All our other boarders were in the living room, gated off, but we could hear them barking every now and then.

Sadie's father was right.

At school, Maggie was the alpha dog and I haven't eaten a real lunch in four months, not since starting middle school. Maggie eats first, of course. One of her pack, Zoe or Larissa or Patrice, always saves her a place in line. She used to be friends with Freida but not anymore.

And it's an unspoken law that they get the long table by the window, close to the salad bar, farthest from the bathroom. The closer you sit to the bathroom the lower you are on the food chain. It would be better if I brought lunch from home, but my mom wants me to buy, so by the time I get my tray of food there is someone at every table.

There is a direct correlation between the amount of time I stand holding my tray looking for a place to sit and how bad my day will be.

"Why don't you sit with us?"

It's the alpha dog.

I'm not stupid. I know this will be a bad idea, but I'd already been standing for thirty, maybe forty seconds, which translates into a very bad day. The feeling will stay with me until I walk in my front door. So I sit down.

"Thanks, Maggie," I say. I plunk my tray down on the table. It's not like we didn't used to be friends back when everyone was friends. When we all got invited to the same birthday parties, like Gabby Fisher-Rees's with the big pool. I bet she'd be at this table if she hadn't moved away. You can just tell.

"Nice poem," Maggie says. "I can see why your mom liked yours better than everyone else's."

Zoe, Larissa, and Patrice all giggle so I figure Maggie had filled them in on what happened in class already. Good news travels faster on a cell phone. Especially with a smartphone and a Twitter account.

Well, so what? When they take their SATs they'll know how stupid they are anyway. But even as I think this, I know it's not true. Besides, Maggie isn't stupid at all. Zoe might be a little on the slow side, but the truth is, I feel really bad for what I said in class.

I'm the stupid one.

"So let us know when you have your first poetry signing," Maggie continues. "We'll make sure to be there."

More giggling, and I wonder what is stopping me from getting up right now. Hunger? Table space? Or the frozen hot feeling in my feet, my legs and my arms and my face, that prevents me from moving at all?

"Oh, sure, we'll be there." Patrice feels the need to add something witty, which she is unable to come up with. "Unless the book smells as bad as you do."

"I can help you with the smelly problem, you know. A little deodorant would go a long way," Zoe says.

Nobody laughs at that one, but nobody tells her to shut up, either.

"Really, Elizabeth. For someone who looks like you do, you really shouldn't be calling attention to yourself. I'm not being mean. I'm just being helpful," Zoe adds.

And yes, a hot feeling can be freezing as in *paralyzing*. I am stuck. I feel like everyone in the cafeteria is watching and listening but I can't even turn my head to see. I squeeze my eyes shut. I try to turn into a chair at the table.

"C'mon, Patrice. I need some chips," Maggie announces, because she can't leave the table without at least one of her entourage. Zoe stands up.

"Me too," she says, even though I know for a fact Zoe wouldn't eat a potato chip or anything that counted as more than five units of fat if her life depended on it.

"Me too." And Larissa follows them because she couldn't bear the experience of possibly being seen sitting at the table alone with me.

Now they are gone and I am no longer a chair. I keep my eyes shut but I can move.

I lean over to Maggie's lunch tray, where an innocent turkey sloppy joe sits, awaiting her return. I gather a satisfactory amount of saliva in my mouth, then carefully and quickly lift the top of her sandwich, spit, and replace the bun, before any of them return to the table.

But when I open my eyes, Maggie throws her back in laughter at something Patrice has said. Zoe laughs even though she hasn't heard what it was. Larissa bites into an apple. None of them has gotten up for chips. No one would be stupid enough to leave their food unattended in the middle school cafeteria.

Nothing has changed.

Nothing ever will.

<u>NO</u> WITNESS TO THE PERSECUTION

Ethan's father had this saying. Well, Ethan's father had a lot of sayings, like: Where there's a will there's a way. Why put off until tomorrow what you can do today? Trust, don't test.

In a very simple way they made sense, and Ethan would nod his head and listen, but all the while he knew his father didn't have a clue about what life was like in middle school.

There is your story and there's my story and then there's the truth, his father would say. This was just another version of the famous, There are two sides to every story.

But he was wrong.

Ethan's father was a banker and he worked with loans, and factors, and numbers, and numbers always added up the same way. People didn't.

Yes, Matthew Berry slugged Stewart Gunderson square in the face, but that wasn't the truth. Not all of it, anyway.

Yes, Stewart Gunderson had it coming. He deserved it. But that wasn't the whole truth either.

And yes, the whole student population was alerted to the incident within a matter of wireless nanoseconds, and that was getting a little closer to the truth.

Matthew was sitting somewhere in the school, waiting for his parents to show up, so they could listen to the guidance counselor relate her version of the truth, which would have been formed with no empirical evidence, but rather, preconceived notions and hearsay.

Or maybe it was just the opposite.

Maybe Mrs. Meadhall was suspending Matthew based solely on empirical evidence, without any consideration of the situation or the backstory of the people involved. After all, Stewart did have a bloody nose and no one could even see the urine that had dried on Matthew's shoes anymore.

Ethan had no idea, but he knew it was unfair.

Life's not fair, his father would say.

Really, Dad? I didn't know that.

Have you been to middle school lately?

DEPARTMENT OF HOMELAND SECURITY

WMS GUIDANCE DEPARTMENT MEMO

TO: All Student Classes
FROM: Jennifer Sansone, Director of Guidance
SUBJECT: Anti-bullying agenda

Our newly implemented "Bully Box" will sit in
the outer area of the main office, next to the
sign-in book on the left end of the counter.
It will be completely anonymous, unless, of
course, you choose, as we strongly advise,
to put your name on your entry. The forms to
fill out will be in a tray to the right of
the box itself. Pencils will be available as
well. All valid complaints will be carefully
attended to, but remember, there is a distinc-
tion between telling and tattling.
To clarify: Tattling is about wanting to get

someone in trouble, whereas telling is about doing the right thing.

We trust our middle-schoolers to know and respect the difference.

Sincerely,

Jennifer Sansone

BULLY BOX FORM

Your name:_____

Grade:_____ Today's date:_____

Please check one:

☐ I am being bullied.　　☐ I have observed someone
else being bullied (bystander).

Bully's name:_____

Date of event:_____

Please describe the event in as much detail as you can (use the back if necessary):_____

_____

_____

_____

_____

Other witnesses:_____

When complete, put this sheet in the Bully Box in the front office for review by a school administrator.

EMPATHY IS OVERRATED

Freida was a strange name to begin with, so maybe it was natural that it belonged to a strange girl. But "strange" was a strong word, wasn't it? *Surprising or unusual in a way that is hard to understand?* No, Freida wasn't really hard to understand. She was different because she wanted it that way, and *that's* what was surprising.

"Why do you have to dress like that? It's like you're just asking for it." The words flew out of Nadine's mouth.

Now, Nadine might have seemed like an unusual or strange name as well, but Freida's sister could have been the poster child for fitting in. If there was a National Month of the Normal Child, Nadine would be the spokesperson. Even her own mother would have a hard time picking out Nadine in her seventh-grade class photo. Nadine blended in like a leaf bug on a leaf, like a flounder on the sandy sea floor.

"Why do you care?" Freida answered her sister. She pushed the door to her bedroom closed with her foot.

"Because you look like a freak and everyone thinks so." Nadine's voice trailed off down the hall and into the bathroom where she would spend anywhere from fifteen minutes to half an hour putting on makeup.

Freida pulled a black sweatshirt that read JUST BECAUSE YOU'RE WEARING BLACK DOESN'T MEAN YOU'RE ONE OF US over her head. She knew no one would get the irony, the double entendre of wearing black herself and not belonging, but she liked the sweatshirt. It was comfortable. It hid her body, hanging nearly to her mid-thighs. It hid her thighs, which had somehow overnight softened and widened and seemed not to fit with the rest of her body.

"Mom," Nadine was now wailing from her bedroom, "I can't find my blue top."

"Did you check in your drawer?" Mrs. Goldstein shouted up the stairs.

"God, Mom. If it was in my drawer I wouldn't be looking for it, would I?"

Freida stood and watched Nadine stepping in and out of pants and throwing sweaters on the floor, flinging shoes across her room. It was like that pretty much every morning until Nadine found something she could wear, usually as their mother called out that she could see the yellow of the school bus through the woods behind their house.

"Did you check under your bed, sweetie?"

"Did you wash it? I put it in the laundry last week. Have you done the laundry in, like, forever?"

Freida gave her sweatshirt a tug and let out a sigh. She would wait for her sister because that's what sisters do, and a few minutes later they were running down their driveway, each with a warm bagel in their hand. They stopped and stood, panting.

"So you never gave me an answer," Nadine said. They could see the bus stopped at the Weavers' house. It took a while for all four Weaver children to board.

"To what, exactly?"

"Freida, I love you. I'm your big sister. I know it sounds mean, but people make fun of you. I'm trying to protect you, but you make it hard. You've got that sixth grade dance coming up, don't forget."

Freida knew her sister loved her. But an if-you-can't-beat-'em-join-'em philosophy didn't work for everyone. It wasn't even working for Nadine.

It was just that Nadine didn't seem to realize it. Maybe in the end, though, not realizing you're *not* "in" amounted to the same thing as being "in."

THE TROUBLE WITH URINALS

"Have you ever been peed on before, ma'am?"[1]

That's what I said, word for word. Not that bad, right? Well, at least I didn't think so. But judging by her reaction you would have thought I had just told her that she looked old or that her office smelled like a weird combination of Lysol and cheeseburgers.[2] Yet, for some reason that question really set her off, kind of like she had been peed on before. And this is when the thought first arose that maybe, just maybe, I wasn't

---

1. I hope I said ma'am. I mean, I think I did. But I always remember myself being politer in my memories. And taller.

2. What? I didn't actually say those things. Just saying that I could have. They were all true.

going to be able to talk my way out of this one.

"WHAT did you say to me, young man? Oh, the inso-lence! You better watch your mouth in my office. You are this close[3] from being suspended from this school. This close.[4] I hope you understand that this is an extremely serious matter, and if you don't start acting accordingly, I will not hesitate to call your parents."

"Oh, no, please don't call my parents, Ms. Meadhall."

I did my best to say that sentence earnestly, although it was difficult because no more than five minutes earlier I had asked her to call my parents. I knew my dad would get a kick out of this whole thing, and my mom, well, I knew she'd hate this woman as soon as she met her. Well, actually, I think she already did hate her, but I knew this whole thing would put her over the top. So, I figured that if I pretended I didn't want Ms. Meadhall to call

---

3. She held up two of her gnarled fingers to demonstrate just how close I was. I appreciated the visual, really I did, but I wanted those disgusting fingers out of my face.

4. Yup, she did it again. For the sake of humanity, get your fingers out of my face, woman.

my parents, then maybe this time, she would call them. Unfortunately, Ms. Meadhall is obtuse in all senses of the word,[5] and that brings us to the biggest predicament in my tale: The woman refuses to listen to a single word I, or really anyone, says.[6]

"I hope you are taking this situation seriously, Matthew. There is a boy in the hospital right now with a broken nose, and he is claiming that you punched him in the bathroom today at lunch. Jason, our security guard, then found you on the road leaving school right after the lunch period ended, clearly with blood on your shirt. So you tell me, Matthew, if you were me, what would you think?[7] Now, please enlighten me as to what exactly happened between you and Stewart today. And this time, Matthew, only the truth."

"Well, I'll say it again, but it's going to be the same story it was when I said it ten minutes ago. . . ."

---

5. Get it? Like an obtuse triangle. She's wide. That makes sense, right?

6. In her defense, this may have been due to the two giant balls of earwax firmly planted in each of her ears. It was like someone had left a candle burning in there overnight. I swear.

7. I would think that I had somehow gotten myself into a situation that is a thousand times worse than the one Gregor Samsa found himself in. Also, I would not have responded nearly as calmly.

I guess it all started in fourth grade, Ms. Perroni's class, my first year at this school. We had moved into town late the previous summer, so I didn't know anyone here. I wasn't worried, though—figured it would take some time to meet people and I would spend that time being under the radar. However, on my first day of class, Ms. Perroni decided to ask me all these questions in front of everyone just because I was the new kid.[8]

She asked me where I moved from, what my favorite subject was, what my parents did for a living, if I had any siblings, you know, all the usual stuff. Nobody in the class seemed to be paying much attention to my responses.[9] But then she asked me what I liked to do for fun and my life changed forever.[10]

---

8. Seriously, though, why do we always do this to the new kid? Oh, hey sonny, nervous on your first day in a new school with no friends? Well, do you want to go up in front of the entire class and be asked oddly personal questions? Oh, no? Not at all? You'd rather sit in the electrical closet all day? Well, let's do it anyway.

9. Which I was thrilled about, by the way.

10. There were so many different things I could have said, so many other things I liked to do for fun. Why didn't I say any of them? It would have made everything so much easier. Video games? Yup, that's a better answer. I bet it still would have turned out better if I had responded with "cooking" or "making origami swans."

Basketball, I told the class, I like to play basketball.[11]

I didn't get it at first. I didn't understand why the class was now suddenly interested, why everyone was suddenly whispering to one another. I couldn't understand why some of the kids were now looking straight at me while others were looking around the classroom, searching for something. No, searching for some*one*.

He was in the last seat in the back of the class, all the way by the door. The first thing I noticed was a fitted hat that lay drooped over his eyes. The front two legs of his chair were floating off the ground as he leaned dangerously backward, with the back of the chair balanced on the rear wall of the classroom. His feet were resting on the empty desk in front of him, spread exaggeratedly wide either for comfort or stability. The last thing I noticed was that there was a basketball in his hands.

"You play ball, huh?"

---

11. Don't get me wrong, I did like to play basketball then. Still do, I guess. I just wouldn't ever have defined myself by the fact that I like to play basketball. And at this school if you say you like to play basketball in the fourth grade, you're claiming that you're Michael Jordan.

I could only manage a nod.[12]

"We'll see about that."

I didn't know he meant that day. At recess he found me and told me that he and the guys play basketball every day on the blacktop. He wasn't really asking if I wanted to play. It seemed kind of like I had to. I still didn't really know yet what I was getting myself into.[13]

It seemed like a normal game. We had 10 kids and we split into two teams. Stewart and some other kid were the captains. Stewart picked first. The kid he chose walked over to his side of the court and they slapped hands. Then the other captain picked and the same thing happened, the selected kid walked over to the other side of the court and they slapped hands. Then Stewart said it.

---

12. I should have said no. Should have said that I misspoke. Basketball? Me? No way. I meant to say Quidditch. Yeah, with the broomsticks and everything. Yup, that's what I do for fun.

13. Unbeknownst to me at the time, I had just entered into a covenant. It was a game in the same sense that Jumanji was a game. Once you're in it, you can't really ever get out.

"I got the new kid."

I walked over to his side. He didn't attempt to slap my hand. He looked me over, from shoes to haircut. He was still looking at me as he picked the rest of his team, watched as I introduced myself to my new teammates and tied my shoes and stretched my legs. I was getting the feeling that this was less of a game than a tryout.

"Let's see what you got, kid."[14]

Maybe I should have sucked that day. Maybe I should have missed every shot I took and dribbled the ball off my knee whenever he passed it to me. Maybe then it would all be different now.[15]

---

14. What I got? I got common sense! Where is your common sense, young Matt? Get out of there. Run! Go hang out in the band room with the band geeks. Go find some science nerds to befriend. Or even just meander on over to the football field and see what's going on over there.

15. He would have made fun of me mercilessly that day, most definitely. Oh, yeah, you play basketball, huh? Nice handle, nice shot, you suck. Get off my court. But then that would have been it. I would have been out of sight for him, wouldn't have mattered.

But I was pretty good at basketball, and I showed it. I played well, I stood out, I impressed people. I wish I hadn't.

You see, Stewart is really good at basketball. I was not as good as him, though, which was lucky because I really can't fathom what would have happened then. But I was good enough.

"Hey, you played all right out there, what's your name again?"

I thought I had found a friend. I guess I did.

I thanked him and told him my name was Matthew and that he played really well too.

"Well, Matty, aside from the fact that you look like a girl when you shoot and those shoes are embarrassing for you to be seen in,[16] I'd say you have some potential."

_____

16. They were Skechers. Embarrassing? I wouldn't say so. If I could go back and put on a pair of shoes that day would I have chosen Skechers again? Highly doubtful.

We walked into the school together. It felt like everyone at recess was watching us. He told me about the Rec basketball league the school ran and how his team was undefeated. Then he made fun of my haircut[17] and slapped my hand as we got near the classroom. The rest of my time in middle school had just been contractually agreed upon.

"All right, Matthew, well, that is right and good and all, a nice story, quite dramatic if I may say, but it has done nothing to tell me about the incident today."

"Yes, yes, Ms. Meadhall, I was just giving you some context. But we can fast forward a year or two if you'd like."[18]

There I am, this morning, sitting at my desk in homeroom, just minding my own business, doing my thing, when Stewart and Scott walked in. They came over and sat down next to me, Scott slapped my hand and said

---

17. To be fair, it was the tragic, yet ever-so-common in middle school, mushroom cut. Why do parents let their kids suffer the humiliation?

18. Or if the buffet is closing soon and you're in a rush.

what up, Stewart slapped my face, gently enough, and said, Good morning, Madeleine.[19]

We had basketball practice right after school that day because there was a band concert in the gym at night, so I had worn my basketball shoes to school. I thought I was being smart, figured I wouldn't have to carry them with me all day in that case. Stewart did not agree.

"Hey, jerk, why do you have your basketball shoes on? You're gonna ruin the soles and mess up the traction. Then you'll fall on your face like an idiot and blow another game for us."[20]

I told him I'd change them, that I thought I had another pair in my gym locker. He told me not to forget to save him a seat at lunch today. I told him I wouldn't. Then we went to our next period class.

When lunch came around, I was already more irritated

_____

19. That was one of his favorites. You get it, because I'm a girl? Matt→Madeleine. Yeah, Stewart is a real thinker.

20. I still don't remember blowing the first one.

than usual. I was on edge. I had just gotten a test back in history class and it did not go nearly as well as I thought it had when I took it.[21] I was sitting at the lunch table, my jacket in its normal place on the seat to my right, serving as a reservation, and Scott sitting in the seat next to that.[22]

We could hear Stewart coming down the hallway toward the cafeteria before he got there. The reverberating sound of a basketball bouncing up and down was an easy give-away.[23] He came in with the basketball in hand, walked over to his designated seat, and sat down, casually shoving my jacket to the ground in the process.

He asked around about what was for lunch today, how the pizza looked, if there were Italian dunkers, and then told me that the sandwich that my mom had made for

---

21. Those are always the ones that get you. If you think you crushed a test and then find out you did anything less than spectacular it will be a letdown. Always have low expectations, y'all.

22. Stewart always had to be in the middle. Of everything. Talk about metaphors, man.

23. The hollow sound that a basketball makes on a middle school hallway is indelible in my mind. It is equal parts terrifying and rousing. Kind of like the bell sound in *Law and Order* or the theme song from *The X-Files*.

me looked disgusting.[24] Then he got up to buy his lunch and told me to come with him. I said I had lunch already but I could get a cookie or something, I guess.

When we were waiting in line to pay, he stood behind me and kept pushing me into the back of the girl in front of me. I kept telling her how sorry I was and telling him to stop. He kept doing it until there was no longer a girl in front of me and it was my turn to pay. I gave the cashier my school card.

"Matthew Berry, huh, kid? Never heard of you, must not buy lunch a lot."

"Actually, he prefers to go by Madeleine."

I told the man no, I didn't, and that yeah, my mom usually makes my lunch. Then I started off back to my seat, but remembered to wait for Stewart. After he paid, we returned to the table where Scott was still sitting with the rest of the guys. I was feeling weird.[25]

---

24. It was tuna fish. It smelled bad. It tasted absolutely delicious.

25. Looking back, I can describe it as the feeling of reaching a tipping point. I'm not sure why but I was nearing it. All these little things were adding up, but they'd never break me. Something much bigger was necessary.

After we all finished eating, Stewart suggested we should go to the bathroom. We were standing at the urinals in our usual positions, Stewart in the middle of me and Scott, when Stewart noticed I hadn't changed my shoes like he said to. He was not happy.

"Why didn't you change out of your basketball shoes, stupid?"

I told him I had forgotten and that I wasn't worried about them getting ruined.

"And that's why you're an idiot. Only wear your basketball shoes when you're playing basketball. You have to change 'em or else you'll screw it up for all of us this weekend."[26]

And then I said a word he probably hasn't heard me say often: No. I said I wasn't going to go outside with them on and that I would be extra careful walking around. What's the worst that could happen to them?

---

26. Oh no, the terror of ruining a sixth-grade travel basketball playoff game! How would I ever have been able to forgive myself?

"Someone could pee on them."

He then pivoted toward me, looked me directly in the eye, flashed a sadistic smirk, and proceeded to urinate all over my shoes and legs. Then he laughed and turned back into the urinal.

"See, like that."

I looked down for a second. My lower body basted in another man's liquid excretion. I looked up. I thought about what had just happened. I looked down again. I looked at Stewart. Still laughing. I looked at Scott. He was silent and didn't return my stare. I looked down again.

I had been peed on. This much was sure. It was a situation I had not thought I would find myself in that day, or pretty much any day. I was ill-prepared to handle it. But really, what would you have done?

I turned to Stewart. I did not say anything. I looked him right in the eyes. He was still smiling. Then I looked down again, made sure he saw me look down. Then I looked back up and punched him as hard as I could right in the face. I think he was still peeing when he hit the ground.

Then I walked out of the bathroom and left the school, and as you have already said, Ms. Meadhall, that is when Jason, the security guard, found me. Now I am here, hoping that this time you actually listened to my story.

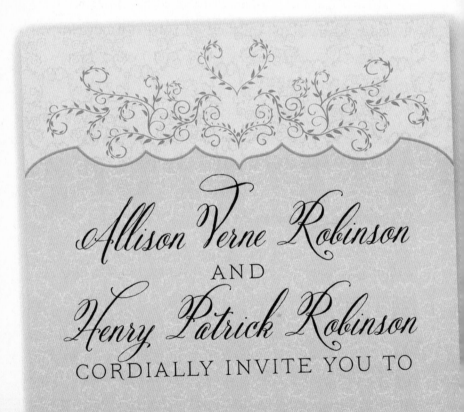

Allison Verne Robinson

AND

Henry Patrick Robinson

CORDIALLY INVITE YOU TO

HURRICANE HELEN

My mother said she wanted to take me shopping for a new dress for Miss Robinson's wedding. She said that, but she also said if it rains during a wedding that's good luck for the marriage, and I find that hard to believe. The ceremony is this afternoon and, of course, no shopping, no new dress. And bad weather is forecast.

The dogs knew it was coming. They huddled around in the kitchen all day, all of them. Patty-Lou didn't want to go outside to pee this morning, even though it wasn't raining.

"C'mon, Patty," I tried, holding open the kitchen door. It was actually sunny and beautiful outside.

The calm before the storm, my mother said, but she was still in bed.

Patty-Lou didn't budge. She was a beagle mix, a hound-ish, long-nosed dog with floppy ears and the sweetest face.

"What's the matter?"

Patty was one of our regulars. She was always comfortable here, but her owners did say she was terrified of thunderstorms, and requested that Patty-Lou get to sleep with one of us if she got scared. My mother promised and then winked at me when Patty Lou's mom wiped her eyes and headed to her car to drive away.

Now I had to get dressed. I had to get ready for Miss Robinson's wedding. I didn't know how many kids would show up, but I wanted a good seat. I wanted Miss Robinson to see I was there, that I made the effort so that she could like me again. I had made a special card for her. My mother said I should make it for both the bride and the groom, but I wanted it to be just for Miss Robinson, so I made two.

I wrote a haiku.

I grabbed Patty-Lou by the collar and yanked her. "Now pee," I ordered. She promptly sat down, making her body as small as possible and looked up at me. If dogs could cry her eyes would be welling up with tears.

"No, no sad-and-puppy face."

Laurie's mother was coming by to pick me up in twenty-five minutes. I pretended not to see Patty-Lou. "Get outside now. I don't have much time."

I know you are not supposed to talk to dogs like that, giving out too much information that they can't understand. It just confuses them. All they hear is noise and they freeze up.

Why didn't I lay out my outfit last night? As if I kept believing my mom and me were going to go shopping, all the way up until yesterday? And then up until dinner? And then all the way until I went to bed and got up this morning, five minutes ago. So I put on my last year's party dress. The one I wore to the spring concert and Aunt Joan's funeral. It's fine.

But now I needed to let out seven dogs and feed them all before I left.

I was late. Everything needed to go perfectly. Everyone needed to understand they had to hurry, eat, and do their business. But it wasn't going to be Patty-Lou, was it? She was just going to make me late and make me look stupid, so I kicked her—hard—in the underbelly of her soft unprepared body.

The sound that came out of her mouth was awful, a high pitched yelp escaped in a whoof of air. Patty-Lou followed her front legs, low to the ground, and moved slowly outside, her tail tucked and her head down. She took a few steps out onto the lawn.

"Oh, no. Oh, no. Oh, no." I ran out into the soggy grass and dropped to my knees. She didn't smell so good, but I wrapped my arms around her little waist anyway. "I am so sorry. I am so so sorry," I said to Patty-Lou.

I was getting grass stains on my dress, on my white tights, but I didn't care.

Our lawn was an embarrassment. Torn up from digging, yellow from pee, dried out. In fact, grass only grew in small patches here and there like a blotchy rash. Patty-Lou slowed down, turning her head as if she didn't want anyone to watch her do her business. Dogs are like that. They like a little privacy even though they'd sit right in front of you and lick their private parts all day if you'd let them. But they like to pee and poo in private.

So I looked away, back toward the house, as soon as I was sure she was squatting down and going. And just like that it started to rain. It was just little drops, hitting the concrete in dark circles. I looked up at the sky, which, when you think about it, is kind of a funny thing to do. It was still sunny outside but the rain pattered loudly. The weatherman on TV was predicting a hurricane. They'd already given it a name. A girl's name.

It used to be that hurricanes were given only girls' names and then someone complained, probably a girl, saying that it gave girls a bad reputation. And now they alternate with boy's names, to try to look fair. And the news was telling everyone to fill their bathtubs with water. *Why?* And to stock up on canned food and flashlights. People who lived near the shore were being advised to leave their homes.

But Miss Robinson's wedding had not been canceled, at least not the ceremony part—that was going to start very soon, any minute now, and Patty-Lou hadn't moved. She was sitting still, waiting for me after she peed, like I held all the answers. Like I could really hurt her if she did the wrong thing. Like I was in charge or something. I saw she was starting to shake, tremble like an egg in a frying pan.

There are some kinds of hurt that are just too much to feel.

AND THEN THERE ARE THE CHICKENS

Jolie liked the monkeys best, so whenever they went to the Bronx Zoo it was the monkey house the whole family trooped to first. It would also be their last stop on the way out at the end of the day. Jolie always loved the monkeys.

It was hard for Stewart, at least when he was younger, that every whim and every wish of his sister's was answered while his remained secondary, even though Jolie was two years older than he was.

"I'm hungry," Stewart complained.

"We're going to eat lunch at the cafe. Just be patient, baby."

He hated being called baby, especially while his sister

was the one in the wheelchair being forwarded, full tilt, to the monkey house.

"But if we don't get to Asia World, there will be a huge line for tickets," Stewart said. He wasn't hungry at all, he realized.

His dad said, ruffling Stewart's hair, "There's plenty of time for everything. We have all day."

They passed the zoo center and took the path to the right. Asia World was to the left.

When he was a toddler, Stewart used to cry that he wanted to ride in a wheelchair too. He would scream and bend his body and arch his way out of his stroller or his father's arms, or just writhe around on the ground. His sister would just watch and shake her head.

Oh, Stew. You don't really want to ride in the wheelchair. You need to appreciate what you have. Your legs, your lungs.

But no matter what anyone said, and long after he stopped whining about it, Stewart wanted to be pushed around in a wheelchair, at least every once in a while. Then he started to notice how people looked at his sister when they went out. They either looked or tried to look like they weren't looking. They were disgusted, he could tell, by her running nose and running eyes, her lolling head. He hated them when they looked, and he hated when they looked away.

He did. He appreciated his legs, and his arms, and his lungs. How he could run faster, faster than most. Participate in gym. Swim and play kickball. His father was so proud of him for making the Biddy-All-Star basketball team in fourth grade. He was unusually athletic, unusually strong for his age. Of course, he appreciated that and he hated himself for it.

"Here we are," Stewart's mother sang out.

"Again," Stewart mumbled, but only his sister heard him.

The Monkey House was one of the oldest original buildings at the zoo. It had huge alabaster pillars flanking its majestic entrance. Just above the door, carved in stone, was the bas-relief of a pensive monkey, resting his arm over his bent knee, staring out at the world. Stewart and his family took the handicapped ramp and pushed their way inside, where the outside world disappeared.

It didn't look quite the same as when it opened in 1901. Now the monkeys lived behind glass, or half-glass walls, in as close to real environments as could be created. Living moss-covered trees, thick hanging vines, moisture-filled air, and monkeys running, jumping, screaming, climbing on branches, and hanging from their tails.

It was crowded with people. Couples with cameras, families snapping pictures with cell phones, people pointing, clapping, ooing and ahhing. Everybody, it seemed, loved the monkeys.

The Internet is rich with monkey videos, especially of monkeys doing nasty things, like peeing on each other, appearing to kiss each other, biting each other, grooming each other, looking and acting as close to human as any animal can. No one knew it then, but by the end of that day, there would be a new video that would go viral within a week and spark an outcry of animal rights activism.

Jolie got out of her chair to stand close to the divide. They were in Madagascar, according to the information plaque. The Squirrel Monkeys were particularly active and vocal, leaping from branch to branch, dipping down close to the body of water below, then flying back up and screaming louder.

One of the monkeys was tormenting the otters who also inhabited this exhibit. The monkey would stealthily climb down his branch, clinging to the wild, fingerlike roots, and slap the otters on the head as they swam by, then scurry back up the tree with glee. It seemed to Stewart that the other monkeys in the trees looked like they were laughing at the otters' misfortune, again and again. But this time there was some kind of scuffle. The crowd pushed closer to see what was going on.

Stewart's mother and father used their bodies and arms to keep people at a distance from Jolie as she watched. The air was thick and humid inside the monkey house. Jolie had her inhaler, but they had to be careful how long they stayed inside.

As Stewart watched, one of the otters had had enough, and with his sharp claws yanked the monkey into the water. Though it took a while for the group of people to realize what had happened, the other monkeys knew immediately. As the monkey in the water thrashed about, fighting for its life, the ones in the trees screamed. Then those on the other side of the glass began wailing as well.

"Oh, my God. Oh, my God. Oh, my God," Jolie said.

"What?" Her mother bent closer.

"The monkey is drowning. Someone has to do something. Somebody do something."

"Call someone. Someone call someone. Someone do something."

But everyone was frozen. You weren't allowed to jump over the glass, into the water. Everyone knew how dangerous that was. Not to mention forbidden. And besides, what could they do? Otters were fierce. They lived on fish and shellfish, which they were expert at opening with their sharp claws and teeth.

One man tried whistling very loudly as if the sound would end the attack, but of course, it didn't. The monkeys leaped higher into the branches, safe but agitated, their shrieking indistinguishable from the humans'. By the time zoo personnel arrived to pull the dead monkey from the water, Stewart's mother and father had pushed their way past the crowd and out the doors.

"Excuse me. Excuse me. Wheelchair. Wheelchair coming through."

They hadn't been back to the zoo since.

Stewart didn't stumble onto the video until two years later, when he was working on a sixth-grade science report about evolution. He saw the footage when he was googling primates on the internet and there it was.

Someone had caught the whole thing on their cell phone and uploaded it to YouTube.

Monkey Dies at Bronx Zoo

People had posted all sorts of comments from, *The monkeys were bullies, they deserved it* to *What kind of horrible people post a video like this? They should be the ones to drown.*

"How's the work going?" Stewart's father poked his head in the door.

"Fine," Stewart answered. He didn't turn around. His face was still a bit swollen. He had two black eyes but the doctor said it was better to wait until he was older to do anything in terms of plastic surgery.

"Look, Stu," his father said. "It's no big deal. You'll get 'em next time."

FOUND IN MIDDLE SCHOOL DUMPSTER AND PARTIALLY EATEN BY A RAT

BULLY BOX FORM

Your name: Fred Flintstone and Barney Rubble

Grade: every grade since 3rd and counting   Today's date: happens all the time

Please check one:

[X] I am being bullied.
(who hasn't?)

[X] I have observed someone else being bullied (bystander).
(In this case, I didn't have to. Everybody knows)

Bully's name: Stewart Gunderson

Date of event: Today

Please describe the event in as much detail as you can (use the back if necessary): Stewart Gunderson picked on Matthew Berry like he picks on everyone all the time and Matthew couldn't take it anymore. All he did was stand up for himself. No one is saying punching someone is a good thing but punishing Matthew is not the right thing either.

Other witnesses:

When completed, put this sheet in the Bully Box in the front office for review by a school administrator.

HERE COMES THE BRIDE

My mother dropped me off in the back of the church and it was a long walk around the block to the front. It was easier to get back there since the main street was one way. It was starting to rain pretty hard.

"Take my umbrella," my mother said.

"No, I'm late, Mom." I stepped out.

"We'll probably need to bring some wood in when you get back," she said as I was shutting the car door. "You sure you can get a ride home?"

My dress shoes were already turning from white to gray.

I nodded yes, but I wasn't sure at all. I hadn't asked anyone from class for a ride home, but I didn't want to miss the wedding. Miss Robinson was mad enough at me, even if she didn't act like it. I had to show up and show her how much I liked her, but I was worried about getting home. I mean, who else would come out in this weather if they didn't have to?

The front rows on both sides of the aisle were all filled up. I should have taken the umbrella. My hair was plastered to my head.

I was hoping to sit with someone from school who lived near me, but there were so few kids there at all. Maggie was there and I saw that she was alone with plenty of room on either side of her. Luckily I saw Freida Goldstein, and I knew Freida lived closer to me, anyway. Maggie lived on the whole other side of town.

If Freida catches my eyes I can sit with her. If she catches my eye I can say hello and then maybe sit down. And then she called out to me first. "Wanna sit here?"

"Sure." I sat down on the hard wooden pew.

"Not many kids from class showed up," Freida said.

"Hey, do you think you can give me a ride home after the ceremony?" I just blurted it out.

Freida laughed, but not a mean laugh.

"We just got here. It hasn't even started yet."

"I know. I just . . . it's just that I don't . . ."

"Sure," Freida jumped in. "My mom loves to drive kids home, but she'll talk and talk and ask you tons of personal questions. Are you all right with that?"

Now I laughed. "Sure."

"I love a wedding. Do you watch that show on TV?" Freida lowered her voice. "*Say Yes to the Dress?*"

The minister guy had started talking. I whispered back. "Yeah, I watch it all the time."

The music started and the wedding party made their way toward the altar. The service went on for a long time, a lot about commitment and honor and the future. Miss Robinson and her husband stayed kneeling so nobody could really see anything but the minister. Or was he a priest?

"I really liked your poem," Freida said, leaning in closer.

I could feel my face turn red. "I don't know why I said that. I mean, said that out loud. About my poem and everything." Just remembering what I said made my stomach twist.

"It's okay," Freida whispered. "It really was the best one. By far."

I took a big breath. "My mother didn't even see it. I don't know why I said that."

"It's okay. Don't worry about it."

So Freida knew the truth now, and somehow it made me feel better just to get that off my chest. But it was too late to get Miss Robinson to like me again. Mrs. Robinson will probably like me even less.

"Thanks," I said.

"You're welcome."

Miss Robinson was standing and Mr. Robinson was putting a ring on her finger, but the sound of the rain made it impossible to hear what was going on up there.

ABSOLUTE POWER ABSOLUTELY

And then the storm arrived. November was so late in the year for a hurricane—a superstorm, they were calling it. Cold air from Canada and a tropical storm racing up the coast from the south. Still, Miss Robinson was kneeling at the altar with her soon-to-be-husband right beside her.

Maggie looked around the church. The front rows were all filled up with family and friends of the bride and groom. The few kids from class who had shown up were here in the back pews. Rain pelted the stained glass. Maggie slouched down against the hard wooden seat.

Zoe had promised she was coming and then texted at the last minute.

My mom says its nuts to go out in this weather. Sorry.

And if that wasn't bad enough, Larissa hadn't even bothered to say she wasn't coming. When the organ music began and the wedding procession started down the aisle and Maggie was still sitting alone, she gave up waiting.

Miss Robinson looked beautiful, Maggie had to say. Her dark hair against her pale skin, her dress was so white and so perfect. She didn't look fat at all. She looked like a princess and boy, was she smiling. But it was the way the groom looked at her that really made Maggie choke up. It was like there was no one else in the room as Miss Robinson walked toward him. They even had a flower girl. Maggie turned around to watch the little girl throw petals, and that's when she saw Freida.

Freida's overprotective helicopter mom drove her daughter in this weather? Oh, well, she did. And now Freida was there, sitting with Elizabeth Moon?

It was a full five seconds of staring back before Maggie realized everyone was sitting straight and looking forward again toward the altar and the father, who had begun talking. During the service, Maggie tried to covertly turn her head back to Freida and Elizabeth. They were sitting close and talking, smiling. They looked happy. The wind was picking up and branches were scraping against the building. But Freida and Elizabeth didn't seem to mind.

Freidabeth? Elizada? No, those both sounded stupid. Freida was stupid. This whole wedding was stupid. And Elizabeth was the dog girl, braggy girl, Miss I'm-smarter-than-everyone girl. Smelly-Girl.

Smelly-Girl. What a perfect name for an indie band.

The father paused a minute when the lights flickered, and everyone held their breath but nothing happened. With the wind and the rain, Maggie couldn't hear a word he was saying anyway.

Smelly girl. A good line in a rap battle.

Or a phony deodorant.

Or a nasty person2person page.

A person2person page. So much better than a Burn Book. *Burn Books are for the dark ages. This is the brave new world of technology.*

Smelly-Girl.

It was harder than she thought and it took a lot more time. Filling in all the details, status, life events, location. Yanking photos off the Internet. But at least she had the real picture that Ethan had e-mailed her so no one would mistake who Smelly-Girl really was.

Angelica had gone home early after her husband called to say a huge tree was down and blocking her normal route. Maggie's mother was downstairs trying to cook. The TV news weather forecasters were behaving like actors with their first big movie break. And Maggie worked diligently and with such focus, she hardly heard the rain, she could hardly remember why she had begun this project in the first place.

Friends was the hardest. Making up enough other false person2person people so that the Smelly-Girl page looked legit and funny. She found photos of dogs and other things that smelled and linked their pages until Smelly-Girl had twelve friends.

"I'll be down in a minute," Maggie called to her mom.

"Better hurry. I made lasagna and it's hot."

Likes.

Maggie found funny person2person pages for Smelly-Girl to "like." Stinky Fish Grill. StinkyFeet Band. Stinky Water bath products.

Her mother called up the stairs again, the lights flickered, and Maggie pressed POST.

Sometime in the middle of dinner, Maggie changed her mind. It was all over the news all the time, wasn't it? Cyber-bullying. Internet predators. They always got caught. No one understood and they looked like the bad guy.

"I sure hope we don't lose power," Maggie's mother said.

Maggie stood up from the table and the lights flickered again. "I gotta run upstairs and do something."

"Maggie, sit down," Maggie's mother said. "How often do you have a homemade meal? Relax. Have you thought about what you are wearing to your first dance?"

Dance? No, Maggie hadn't thought about that at all. She took the stairs two at a time. She flipped open her laptop and watched her screen come up. She frantically opened to person2person just as the power went out. Electricity. Water. Cable. Modem. Internet.

All over town. All over the state. For a full ten and a half days.

WHO'S TOP DOG NOW?

Just because the Israelites took forty years to cross the desert doesn't mean I can live without the Internet for one second longer and, frankly, I have no idea what my dad is talking about anyway.

So what's the worst part?

The water.

Or lack of it, rather.

We haven't been able to flush a toilet without using our water containers that we have to fill up every day and lug into the house. I have to brush my teeth by pouring water from a cup over my toothbrush. My mom gave up trying to cook with water from the bottles and now we just get takeout for dinner and she set up one of those

Dunkin' Donuts coffee dispensers right on the counter next to all the dirty dishes we can't wash. But seriously, the toilet situation is the worst.

And no heat.

No TV.

No Internet.

Did I mention the toilets?

And for some reason that only God or Verizon would be able to explain, no cell service. No talking. No texting. No tweeting.

No toilets.

"I'm cold," my sister says for the ten millionth time in the last hour.

"We all are, Nadine," my mom answers. "Put on a second pair of pants."

But I know she won't, because it will make her look fat even when it's just us who can see her. I, on the other hand, am wearing pajama bottoms, fleece sweatpants, two pairs of socks, a thermal undershirt, a long sleeve T-shirt, a polar fleece jacket, and my dad's ski vest. Oh, and a hat.

School has been closed for four days. We take our showers at the Y.

We do have a small gas heater so we, all four of us, sleep on air mattresses in the den. My mom has—count them—six carbon monoxide detectors set up around the room.

"Daddy snores," Nadine says. She's tucked in her sleeping bag like a knish. I can smell her aloe nighttime facial cream from here.

"Go to sleep, Nadine," my dad says.

We go to bed real early these days. By nine o'clock we've read as much as we can. There's just nothing to do. I haven't gone to bed before ten thirty since I was in elementary school when my dad used to scratch our backs and tuck us in at night.

"Tell us a story, Daddy," I say. I am wrapped up warm, laying between my sister and my mom and dad. I look straight up, watching the lights from the passing cars outside rush across the ceiling and down the side wall.

Nadine groans but we all ignore her.

My dad is the best storyteller. Everybody knew it. Whenever I had a friend sleep over, I would plead with my dad to tell us a bedtime story, and he would pretend to resist until even my friend was begging him. I think my friend Maggie loved his stories more than anyone. Her dad works in Washington, DC, and she doesn't see him very often.

"All righty, then," my dad begins. "Once upon a time . . ."

I haven't been friends with Maggie since last year. She kind of changed groups or maybe I did. Either way I haven't been friends with Maggie since last year.

A year ago she never would have been friends with someone like Zoe, and then it seemed like one day, she just was. I never liked Zoe. She scared me and I knew enough to stay away from people who scared me. But not Maggie, so when Zoe invited five girls to her sleep-over—one of them was Maggie and one of them was me—I didn't want to go.

"Freida, please. You have to go. I can't go without you. We are twins, remember? BFFs. At least do it for me."

I knew why Maggie wanted to go so badly. It was like winning the lottery, like getting a chance to see a live Taylor Swift concert from the front row. It was an offer that wouldn't come again if you didn't act quickly. A chance to stay at Zoe Bellaro's McMansion. Zoe's mother had supposedly been in an episode of *Law and Order* or *Cold Case*. I guess that's kind of cool.

"I don't want to, Maggie. She only invited me because she invited you."

We were sitting on the swings, like we always did, outside the intermediate school. Next year would be middle school, but for now we were safe.

"So, see, that just shows how nice she is," Maggie said. "She's being nice."

I stopped rocking my feet back and forth and looked at my best friend. I knew something was changing.

"Maggie, there is nothing nice about Zoe and you know it. Last week she accidentally on purpose dumped a Pixy Stix in my hair. Why do they sell those things in school anyway?"

I must admit I didn't anticipate Maggie rising to the top of the middle school popularity heap the way she did, but if you ask me, a caged hamster spinning in a wheel is still a hamster, in a cage.

"Along the way, they encounter many obstacles," my dad went on. It's a baby story but my dad's voice is deep and slow.

"Freida, you have to come. You just have to," Maggie

begged me. "If you don't I may have to invoke the BFF emergency rule."

She really wanted me to go with her, but it was a mistake. Zoe didn't like Maggie any more than she liked me. She would do mean things. And then talk about it the next day. I just knew it.

"Then I have to invoke it too, Maggie," I said. "I can make you do one thing I really need you to do even if you don't want to. I don't want you to go to that sleepover."

"And I want you to go with me to that sleepover." Maggie got off her swing and stood on the grass.

It was a standoff, and the end of our friendship. I miss Maggie. We were the Two Musketeers. Was it me or Maggie who made those delicious oatmeal chocolate chip cookies for the bake sale and then we both got belly aches eating them all? Who fell off the swings in second grade and cut her knee wide open?

I have to reach down, under the covers, and under my pajama pants, and touch my skin, to remember. I have a raised scar just above my shin.

It was me.

• • •

"So Gloria and Rabbit sat down by the side of the road to rest," my dad is saying.

He is coming to the end of his story. I feel my eyes closing. I can feel the warmth coming from the heater and from the bodies next to me. I think this is how people were meant to live. I mean, it feels natural, like the way we were in the wild, before electricity and television and Internet, like animals, close together for protection.

When I turn my head, I see my mom and dad. My mom's head is resting on my dad's forearm and Nadine is fast asleep. I hear her slow breathing.

INSIDE OF A DOG

The smells were everywhere in this place, indicating the passage of time, disclosing the identity of the others, revealing details about their age, what they just ate, where they had traveled, both recently and in the past. Junior sat shyly in the corner and watched.

Vision wasn't his favorite means of gathering information, but he didn't dare move any closer to the other dogs. He was new and had to learn his place. No, waiting was the best thing. Watching. Listening. Waiting.

Junior lifted his snout and flared his nostrils, the older air swirled within the inside of his nose while he drew in a new breath. In this way, he could compare the scents—the strength, the quality, the pungency—and tell time.

There was a lot he could learn right from here. The larger of the two humans, the one that seemed to be in charge, was standing in the room where the food smells came from. But Junior wasn't sure. She had the louder voice and she was the one using the tools that humans use to prepare food, but it was the younger one who the other dogs followed with their eyes, and their ears, and their noses. Junior turned his attention to her.

She was female. Of that, he was certain. She seemed kind, though Junior could sense a tension about her, an uncertainty. She was worried about something.

"Hi, Junior." She bent down beside him. "Why are you hiding in the corner?"

She put her hand out, palm flat, a foot or two away from him. She smelled of soap, maybe maple syrup, but *that* was older, metal, the handle of a door. She smelled strongly of the dog she had just been rubbing and that dog smelled of grass, the inside of a car, fresh meat of some kind, a much older odor from another human altogether. Junior tipped his head down and looked away.

The girl understood this to be a friendly sign; she reached over and scratched him behind his ears, in just that, oh, wonderful, spot, yes, just hard enough to feel so good.

"I know you're sad, but you're lucky you're here," the human girl said. "Most everyone else in town has no power, no water. No heat. At least we can cook food here."

Junior cocked his head, lifted his ear, and listened. A word or two made sense: Water. Food.

At the same time he kept an eye and his nose primed for movement behind her. The other dogs were watching too, listening. Whenever a new dog enters the pack, everything is up for grabs. All systems were tensed for change and rearranging.

"But we don't have Internet or TV," the girl went on. She made herself comfortable on the floor beside him. Junior might have gotten up and moved away. He didn't want to show his colors yet, he wasn't ready. He didn't want to look like he was taking the human girl for himself. That might make the others worried or even angry. But she was stroking him, his belly now, and he couldn't move if he wanted. His eyes lowered involuntarily and his throat generated a low, pleased rumble of sound.

"Oh, you like this, do you? Well, I can't stay long, you know. My mother is taking me to the library in town. They are the only ones with Internet, and I've got to check my e-mail."

Junior felt her heartbeat quicken when she spoke those words. Though he didn't know what she said, he knew it was important to her.

"I know you know we don't have electricity because of the hurricane. We are lucky to have a wood-burning stove, so that's why you are warm. My mother promised me she'd take me to the library today because they have Internet there, for some reason. But it's probably going to be crowded, so I want to get there soon."

None of the sounds that were coming from her mouth were comprehensible to him, but a distinct scent rose from her body, from her skin: fear? anxiety? excitement? Junior couldn't precisely tell.

One of the dogs had stepped toward them. He, it was he. Junior could smell his maleness in the air before him. But he wasn't aggressive. He was curious. The way he looked away, the way his tail moved slowly back and forth low to his body but not between his legs. Junior had to look away. It was respectful. This dog had been here first.

"Oh, Poppy. You came over. Poppy, this is Junior. Junior, Poppy. You're both here for a week, so make friends and play nice."

The human girl was smart. She stood up and moved

out of the way. She allowed the two dogs space to move around each other, sucking in air, poking their noses as close to the source as the other would allow. There was so much to know about a new friend, so much history and so much potential.

"Elizabeth," the other human, the older one, called out. "Time to go. You ready?"

The girl gave each of the dogs a rub on the top of their heads. Junior liked it. They both did.

"Off to the library."

She sounded cheerful, but there was something here to be wary of. It wasn't a smell or a movement Junior could see outside. It wasn't a sound he could hear. It was just a sense, the way he knew when his *own* human was on his way home, long before he saw the car or heard any footsteps on the walkway, or smelled his boy's wonderful, familiar scent. Something was going to happen and it wasn't good.

PC

The town librarians weren't at all prepared for the crowds, although they probably should have been. They were the only Wi-Fi hot spot in a fifty-mile radius. They had lights, running water, and cable Internet service. Mr. Werner had called in both Mrs. Frances Greely and Ms. Laura Charles to work that day. Every computer terminal was in use, with a long string of names on the waiting list. Those waiting were supposed to sit quietly and read, but there simply weren't enough chairs. The restrooms were a mess, and the noise alone could have sent any one of the librarians to the madhouse.

"That's a very outdated term, Fran."

"What is?"

"*Madhouse*. You know. Lunatic asylum. That's so eighteenth century."

"Laurie, it's an expression, not a politically correct statement, for goodness sake. It's just mayhem in here. I think every single middle school and high school student from the whole district is here." Mrs. Greely was checking in books from the return bin. You never knew what you were going to find pressed in those pages, the things people used as bookmarks and then forgot to remove before returning.

"Hmm, you're right. And considering half the town has left or is staying in hotels, this is pretty crazy. What are these children looking *up*, anyway?"

Mrs. Greely flipped through the pages of the *Larousse Encyclopedia of Mythology*, Prometheus Press, New York, 1959, before she put it on the cart to take it back to the stacks. There seemed to be some new stains on the fabric cover—they didn't make books like this anymore—but otherwise it was fine.

"For the life of me, I can't imagine," Mrs. Greely answered. She lifted out the next book and gave it a little shake. "Their e-mail?"

"Kids don't e-mail any more," Ms. Charles said.

"They check their person2person page. They listen to music and watch videos."

"Oh."

"And they don't talk on the phone. They text."

"Oh, I know."

"Or Twitter."

"Twitter?"

"I mean, look at that girl over there." Ms. Charles pointed. "She hasn't moved in eighteen minutes. She's just staring at that screen like a zombie."

"She certainly is transfixed, isn't she?"

Mrs. Greely pulled out the next book, *A Candle in Her Room* by Ruth M. Arthur, Aladdin Books, 1966. It had been one of Mrs. Greely's favorite books when she was a child, and she wondered who had taken it out to read.

"Well, she can't sit there much longer, and I sure hope she read the sign about the thirty-minute maximum computer time. I hate having to remind these people."

The book was so magical. It was scary and romantic, suspenseful and mysterious. It was everything a book could or should be. Mrs. Greely held it tight to her chest as if her love for the book could seep into it, out of her heart. Or perhaps it was the other way around.

"Fran? Are you listening to me?"

"Yes, of course, Laurie. You hate to have to remind the kids when their turn is up. I'll do it."

Mrs. Greely slowly tilted the book down and studied the cover. It was the same sketchy illustration she remembered, of a girl in a sweater poking a stick into high leaping flames. The same crinkly plastic paper over the dust jacket. Oh, yes, the doll. There was a magical, evil doll named . . . named Dido. She had been so enraptured by the book that she wanted to own it. She wanted it to be hers.

She loved it so much she had memorized the first and last sentence:

I suppose if we had not come to Prembrokeshire, Judith, Briony and I, this story would never have been written. There would have been no Dido.
Suddenly, I felt secure with a happiness I had never expected to have known, a gentle glowing happiness which burnt inside me like a clear steady flame.

But it was a library book, and it had to go back.

"Well, good, then. You do it this time. But give her

another five minutes or so to stare at the screen."

Mrs. Greely looked up. "What? Oh, sure. Another five minutes."

And you couldn't steal a book from the library because that would be very wrong. Everybody knew stealing a book from the library was wrong, no matter how much you wanted it. No matter how much you loved books and loved being around books and loved this book more than any other.

"My goodness, what *is* that girl looking at?" Ms. Charles went on. "She almost looks like she's going to cry."

But of course, if no one in the library was watching because the librarian was helping someone with the card catalog, thumbing through those stiff rectangular cards . . . and in those days, there were no metal strips. No security systems. No alarms—it was easy.

"You know, Fran," Mrs. Greely said, holding up the book to her colleague, "I didn't even know we had this book in our library."

"What is it?"

"*A Candle in Her Room,* by Ruth M. Arthur. I have the same exact book at home, isn't that amazing?" And when she said that, the top of her head tingled the smallest bit. Was it shame? Or excitement? She didn't know. "I read it as a little girl. I loved it so much, I read it to my campers when I was a counselor at 4-H, and I had both my girls read it when they were young."

"Oh, really? Did they like it too?" Ms. Charles asked, but kept one eye on the clock. "Nearly five minutes."

Mrs. Greely stopped babbling on about the book. It was silly, after all. It was just a book. The girl on the computer was clearly crying—not sobbing so that anyone noticed, only a steady stream of tears was rolling down her face, almost invisible.

But she must have read the thirty-minute maximum sign. The girl stood up, pushed back her chair carefully, then leaned forward and pressed the sign-off button on the keyboard.

"I hope she's okay," Mrs. Greely said, watching as the girl headed back toward the biographies.

"Who?" Ms. Charles said. "It's so noisy in here, I can't hear myself think."

THE CRUCIBLE

"Are you okay?"

Elizabeth looked up from where she was sitting, cross-legged, on the carpeted floor behind the nonfiction stacks, Biography/SP–TS. Funny, she didn't know Ethan that well, even though they'd been in the same class since kindergarten. They probably had never spoken directly to each other, not once before.

"No," she heard herself saying. She was feeling one of those kinds of moments when nothing seems entirely real. How had she gone from being so thrilled, seeing her poem in the anthology, to humiliating herself in front of Miss Robinson, to sitting with Freida at the wedding, to feeling the ground fall out from under her when she came across the person2person page with her picture.

It took Elizabeth a long time to even comprehend what was going on.

She saw the photo.

That was her face, at least it looked like it was. But that wasn't her name. It was a mean name. It wasn't true, was it? The horror of it slowly began pressing in on her lungs and heart. Her breathing quickened but her air supply diminished. Before she could read the profile of this unknown but familiar face, Elizabeth scrolled down to the posted comments. There weren't that many, but there were enough, all from different names with odd person2person profile photos, famous athletes, to dogs, to movie stars.

No one seemed real but they all had something to say about Smelly-Girl. She felt her mind lifting out of her body until she was nearly watching herself at the computer terminal, staring. The Elizabeth that floated above was safe, while the one in the chair began to cry.

"Elizabeth?" Ethan said. He rested his hands on his knees to be closer. To see if she was still breathing.

"Did you see it?" she asked him.

• • •

The voices in the library were loud, but they were distant. The sounds were amplified like millions of fingernails scratching a chalkboard, not making any sense, not human, not real. Far away.

It was then Ethan realized what had happened. It was the fake person2person page that Maggie had made. She published it right before the storm, and it stayed there just long enough for most everyone to see it before the power went out. Elizabeth must have just seen it.

"Yeah, I did," Ethan said softly.

"Why?" Elizabeth asked.

Ethan noticed her face was marked with tear streaks and when he did, he put it together. He shot the photo. He was the reason this girl was crying.

"It was a mistake," Ethan answered. "I didn't know what it was for. She asked me. I didn't know what it was for."

Elizabeth seemed confused. "What?"

"Nothing. I mean, I don't know. I don't why *they* do that. *She* did it. Why *anyone* would do that. Are you okay? I mean, that's stupid. I keep asking you that."

Ethan let his legs give out and he slid down onto the

floor beside Elizabeth. It was strange to be this close to her—well, to any girl, really—but here on the floor, alone but with all these people around. It was the same face as in the photo but it wasn't. The photo was flat, two-dimensional. It didn't feel, it didn't see, it didn't hear.

Here was the same face, alive, crying, knowing all those people had made fun of her and called her names.

Funny names. Funny jokes. Ethan had tried to guess who was who, which of his friends had used an Adam Sandler profile picture, who had used a SpongeBob cartoon. But not once had he thought of this face, of Elizabeth's face, and how she would feel when she saw it.

"Look, it's just stupid. It's just some dumb joke. It could have been on anyone. Just stupid kids being stupid."

Ethan felt only the tiniest relief that he himself had not posted a comment. It wasn't fair. Was that how Matthew felt sitting in the principal's office? Getting in trouble for something someone else did. Something Stewart did.

"But it was me," Elizabeth said. Her body looked so crumpled. "Not someone else."

"Well, you know what they say?" Ethan said.

It was such a beautiful day out, as it had been nearly every day since the storm. Unseasonably warm, almost balmy, and the sun was shining like early spring, not late fall. As if the natural world had no idea how much damage it had done to human society.

"No, what?" Elizabeth could barely lift her head, but she did. She was looking for anything, and she was looking to Ethan to find it.

"Well, they say, Don't get mad, get even."

"They do?" She wiped her eyes.

"Well, I think they also say, Revenge is a dish best served cold."

"What does that mean?"

Ethan didn't really know. He shrugged.

"You think I should get revenge? How? On who?" That's when Elizabeth realized everybody knew who had made the person2person page.

She figured she had only one guess. "Was it Maggie?"

Ethan didn't even have to answer that question.

"Jeez, I didn't say that," Ethan said.

"You didn't have to."

"Anyway, two wrongs don't make a right, you know." Another saying of his father's.

Two huge tears seemed to just appear and drop out of Elizabeth's eyes. "There are a lot more than two wrongs in this world," she said.

Ethan had to agree with that.

HOUSE ARREST

Okay, let's see here. Can we talk this one out? Just bear with me for a second. Yeah, just a second.

Why?

Because. Well, because I think I must be going crazy.

So, okay—you still with me? Okay, good— so, okay, this morning, when I woke up, I came to the abrupt realization that it wasn't actually, technically the morning anymore. I knew this because my room was covered in sunlight. Just bathed in it. It was blinding and confusing and I didn't know what to do.

You know how sometimes you wake up on the weekend and forget what day it is and think that you are late for school and get completely frantic for a second and wonder what chain of events could have possibly led you to forget to set your alarm clock when you never forget to set your alarm clock? And then you realize that it's Saturday and that you can sleep all day if you want to and that you don't have to worry about missing school or if there could be any homework that you may have forgotten to do or if you are going to see He-Who-Must-Not-Be-Named on your way to homeroom today?

Well, that was me this morning. Except it was Tuesday. And school was still going on.

Now, you ask me—yes, I know you didn't really ask me, just go with it— you ask me, why, Matthew, did you wake up at noon, on a Tuesday, when we all know that you wake up at 6:12 a.m. every school day so you can have enough time to shower, have breakfast, watch a little bit of SportsCenter, and still be able to get to class on time?

Aha. It's that last part that is the kicker. There is no class.

Not for me. Not anymore. Because I got peed on and then I got suspended.

Yes, you heard that correctly. I am not allowed to go to school. Not even if I wanted to. Take that.

But I will not let them, the enemy, get me down. No way, not on my watch.

Just because there is no school, I will not change my morning routine, even if it was technically the afternoon.

After I woke up, I immediately took a shower because I always take a shower immediately after I wake up and I don't understand people who don't and are still able to function and engage in everyday life interactions.

Then, after I got out of the shower, I put on my old pair of Power Ranger pajamas—What? Nobody was around, and they are still comfortable—and plopped down on the couch. I was in it for the long haul.

My mom brought me eggs and bacon and a cup of coffee,

wrapped me in a blanket, and asked me if I needed anything else. My dog, Eli, was laying at my feet. The TV remote was in my hands and it had full batteries, while both cabinet doors, miraculously, were open so that the cable box could be reached. I then put on SportsCenter because SportsCenter is always on.

By this time it was probably one in the afternoon. I should have been in humanities class, sitting next to Cady Meshnick, who lets out what she considers to be silent farts all class long and thinks nobody realizes. I'm on to you, Cady, just know that. I see through your game.

What? Oh, well, that brings me back to my original point.

You see, I must be crazy. They told me that I was in trouble. That I'm suspended and that this is supposed to be punishment. This, here, being at home.

But this is awesome. I love this.

I'm away from all that. Away from silent farts and oblivious teachers and people who pee on other people. Away from the schoolwork and the weird janitor who always lingers too long around me and the convoluted web that is the middle school social scene.

I'm away from all that crap.

I wish I could get peed on all the time. Well, I probably take that back. But, three days of no school, sleeping in as late as I want, and playing video games all day, well, that ain't half bad. I could get used to this life.

So you ask me—Matthew, how are your parents handling all of this? They are fine with you sleeping in and doing nothing all day? Isn't that too good to be true?

I'm glad you asked.

So, let's see, "the incident" happened Monday at lunchtime. (I've taken to calling it "the incident," by the way, because it's easy to say and catchy and makes me sound like I actually did something bad.) And then my parents found out about it Monday in the late afternoon, after Mrs. Meadhall finally came through on her bluff to call them.

And they reacted just as I expected. I take that back. They reacted exactly the opposite of what I expected. They were furious, but not at me.

It was my mom who came to school to pick me up. My dad was at work. He didn't find out until later, and his reaction is not exactly fit to print.

"Did you even get my son's side of the story?" Me, my mother, and Mrs. Meadhall sat in the principal's office with the door closed.

"Yes, of course we did," Mrs. Meadhall said.

My mother hadn't even had time to hear my side of the story. I had to sit here and wait for her to show up. I figured she was going to be really mad at me for getting in trouble. I sunk as low in my chair as I could as Mrs. Meadhall told her I punched Stewart Gunderson in the face. I was somehow able to interject *why* I had punched Stewart Gunderson in the face.

My mother didn't even blink an eye. "Well, clearly there's more to the story. Is Stewart Gunderson getting punished?" my mother said.

"That is not something you need to concern yourself with, Mrs. Berry."

"But this isn't fair. Matthew didn't start it. Did you hear what he just said?"

Mrs. Meadhall didn't answer. Instead, she just kept repeating the same sentence over and over. "We do not tolerate fighting of any kind at this school."

"And getting urinated on is not fighting?" my mother tried. I have to give her credit. She probably wanted to use another word altogether.

Mrs. Meadhall was silent.

"This is a done deal, isn't it?" my mother finally said. "You didn't call me in here to talk about this—you've already suspended Matthew, haven't you?"

Mrs. Meadhall was super quiet. Then she admitted, "Yes."

"Let's go, Matty." My mother stood up and as I told you before, my father's reaction wasn't as accepting, but there wasn't anything he could do either.

I haven't been allowed back since.

And to tell you the truth, it really sucks.

Preston Middle School

100 School Road

Preston, New York

Principal Meadhall

Dear Parents,

As our Preston school district returns to its regular
schedule this coming Monday, there are several issues I
would like to address. First and foremost is our children's
safety. The police and fire department assure me that all
the roads have now been cleared of downed trees and
power lines and that our school buses will be able to
move freely on their routes.

After careful consideration of the available options, the
Board of Education and I have decided to cancel spring
vacation in order to make up the days missed during
the blackout. We realize that many of the student body
and their families may have had travel plans during this
time, but we expect full attendance. We have all been
inconvenienced, and this change in the calendar is minor
in comparison to what others have had to contend with
due to Hurricane Helen.

Lastly, we want to remind parents that the first sixth grade dance of the year, sponsored by the Preston Middle School PTO, will go on as scheduled. It will be held Friday night in the Middle School gym from 7:30 p.m. until 10:00 p.m. There will be chaperones at the entrance to the building and no students will be allowed to enter after 8 p.m. or leave before 10 p.m. without special written permission from their parents. Anyone found with prohibited substances (see: Preston Student Handbook, pages 13–16) will be immediately and severely dealt with.

Have a great week,

Mrs. Grace Meadhall

SPIKING THE BALL

Elizabeth had a million ideas flying through her head keeping her awake. Well, she had seven that might work. Okay, she had three real plans for getting back at Maggie. Two that were in any way doable—if she had superpowers. Still, lying in bed planning outrageous evil deeds was the only way Elizabeth could even imagine how she was going to go back to school Monday after seeing the Smelly-Girl person2person page, though it had mysteriously disappeared.

Funny, watching the night doesn't stop the sun from coming up, but when Elizabeth heard the sounds of court TV coming from downstairs, she knew she must have fallen asleep at some point and now it was morning.

The worst morning of her life. Breakfast waiting for her.

"Everything all right?" her mother asked.

Elizabeth tried to swallow a spoonful of cereal. Better yet, she used her mouthful of milk and Cheerios to muffle her answer. "Sure, Mom."

She hadn't told her mother about the person2person page but her anxiety about going to school today was probably obvious. Elizabeth wasn't sure if she was more embarrassed to tell her mother or more worried that her mother might go into the school and make a big stink, which, of course, would only be more embarrassing. In the end she opted for lying.

She finished another spoonful. "No, really. I'm just a little rushed, that's all."

And wouldn't you know it, the bus *was* late, meaning everyone in homeroom would already be seated and they would be halfway through attendance. There was a moment Elizabeth stood outside the door, peering in through the tiny rectangular window. If she could have disappeared, or combusted spontaneously, never to be heard from again, she wouldn't have objected. But with neither of those options presenting themselves, Elizabeth opened the door and walked in.

No one looked up. There was no audible whispering or people who deliberately avoided glancing her way. One foot followed the other, and Elizabeth took her seat by the bookshelves near the back and tried to breathe.

Homeroom was followed by first-period gym, and somehow Elizabeth found herself in the locker room alone. No one had said anything yet or even looked at her differently, but then again the day had only just started.

Lots of kids tried to opt out of P.E. class, especially for the swimming unit, but the physical education department was cracking down on fake notes from home and other excuses. By this time of year, nearing winter break, the sixth grade was well into their volleyball unit, and everyone was expected to participate. Elizabeth could hear Mr. Hill calling out names for the two teams and reminding everyone about the rules.

Rules.

What rules?

Elizabeth bent her knees, sank down between the benches, and let her back press against the cold metal of the gym lockers. She had changed into her P.E. clothes—shorts and a T-shirt—but she couldn't bring herself to go out there. Homeroom was one thing, but a full-period class. No, not yet.

Maybe not ever. Her body felt like it had no bones. You can't bump pass a volleyball or block a shot if you have no bones. That's when Elizabeth noticed the bright pink straps sticking out from the locker directly in front of her. No doubt that was Maggie's backpack. She must have slammed the door shut and not realized that it hadn't locked properly.

Elizabeth looked around, toward the gym door and back to the main entrance and the hallway outside. Quiet. The inside of the locker room was silent. Sounds from the gym class were echoing in the gym. Mr. Hill's whistle shrieked. The volleyball game had started and Elizabeth crawled carefully across the floor toward Maggie's locker, which was ever-so-slightly open.

I was just pushing the straps back in, Elizabeth heard inside her head.

My contact popped out and I was looking for it down here.

Oh, I just lost an earring.

Elizabeth didn't wear contacts or earrings, but who knew that?

Elizabeth carefully pulled open the door and even more carefully unzipped the top of Maggie's backpack, not moving it an inch from its crumpled spot at the bottom of the locker. What could she find inside?

Information is the new weapon. That's what they say these days.

Or was it the new currency?

Elizabeth wasn't sure, but she definitely needed a weapon. A shield, at least. Something to give her the strength to face her friends, face anybody, hold up her head and just make it through the day without wondering what everyone was really thinking about Smelly-Girl.

What a mean thing that was to do. Smelly-Girl. What an evil, awful, mean thing. And nobody was going to do anything about it. Because nobody else was hurt by it. And now it was taken down from the Internet anyway.

Elizabeth let her fingers be her eyes as her hand moved around inside the bag. A long, smooth, cylinder. ChapStick. Skinny, pointy. Ouch. A sharpened pencil. Gum. Bejeweled cell-phone case. Water bottle. Eww, a mushy powerBar. And something folded, folded, and folded again tightly. Elizabeth drew it out. As if it were an ancient text on parchment, she slowly unwrapped it from itself.

It was a letter. In Maggie's handwriting. Well, Elizabeth assumed it was Maggie's handwriting since her name was signed at the bottom. The paper was worn into so many creases but it was still legible.

And oh, wow, jeez. Oh, no. Wow. Look who it was written to.

If information was the new currency, then a love letter to a teacher was a winning lottery ticket.

THE GREEK CHORUS

"Okay, practice is over. Stretch out. I'll be in my office . . ."

We didn't know if Coach Fogden had actually said those words or if we had just been wishing he'd say them for so long that we, together, had made the sentence magically become audible. It could have been a group hallucination. We didn't know for sure, so we kept running.

There's a certain sound that a group of basketball players in a gym makes after they have been running for two straight hours. The time between steps is shorter. Your legs feel so heavy that they're really being dragged more than lifted. You can no longer make out the sound of distinct footsteps hitting the floor. It becomes more of a group-shuffling noise.

Sh-sh-sh-sh-sh-sh.

But over and over again. Up and down the court. Everywhere.

Sh-sh-sh-sh-sh-sh.

Oh, and don't forget the breathing. The loud, labored, painful breathing, in various rhythms coming from all over the court. And the coughing, and the spitting, and the occasional throwing up of a sandwich that was eaten too close to the start of practice.

But mostly it's the sound of shoes shuffling on hardwood.

Sh-sh-sh-sh-sh-sh-sh.

Touch the line and run back. Touch the next line and run back to the first line. Touch all the lines and don't stop running. Ever.

Coach Fogden gleefully calls them "suicides." That's

what we are running. We are running suicides. We think we might be allowed to stop, but again, we may be hallucinating.

We finish the suicide and look up. We scan the gym. We blink and rub the sweat out of our eyes.

Coach Fogden is gone. He's no longer in the gym. He is in his office, like he said. We weren't hallucinating. Practice is over. We are supposed to stretch out now.

We look at each other. Normally there are twelve of us, but today there are ten.

We have our hands on our knees, our torsos bent over our legs, and we're sucking in breaths of air so rapidly that it might appear to an outsider that we are all competing over a limited amount of it.

The breaths are loud because they are urgent. It is the only thing we can hear. We need that air.

Whoooo-woo whooo-woo whoo-woo.

Then we all fall to the ground. Just start collapsing. One after another, right in the exact spot where we stopped running. It can't really be called sitting on the ground, because we don't sit. Sitting requires controlled movement. We have no controlled movements anymore.

We crumple.

To the ground.

Nobody says anything. Nobody can talk.

The first thing that goes when you have been running for that long is your ability to speak. Even if you are somehow able to open your mouth, which requires muscles that you no longer have the strength to use, you have another problem: the fact that you don't have any saliva left in your mouth.

You aren't going to be able to produce any sounds with a mouth as dry as the Sahara.

That's what Coach Fogden told us the last time he made us run and not stop. It was after someone had talked back to him. He told us we were going to run until we couldn't talk anymore. And then we'd see if anyone spoke back to him.

That was a month ago and now it was happening again.

Only our offense was much worse this time. Or so he told us. We still aren't really sure what we did. How could *we* have stopped Matthew from punching Stewart?

All Coach Fogden said was, "I don't care what happened. All I care about is that now Stewart can't practice."

And then he yelled "SEW-AHHHHH-CIDES." So we started running.

And now we are here, countless suicides later, crumpled on the floor, attempting to breathe normally again.

Whooo-woo whooo-woo whoo-woo.

Eventually some of us are able to get up, get some water, Gatorade, any kind of liquid, and slowly begin stretching.

Normally Stewart would start us off. We'd get into a circle at center court and he'd call out each stretch as we went through them, but without him there we are more than glad to make do on our own.

Nobody needs to count to ten out loud. It's not necessary.

But the silence was killing us. The only noise we could hear was one of us bouncing a basketball, playing around with it as he was stretching.

Bom-bom, bom-bom, bom-bom.

The silence was draining. Someone needed to say something. Our saliva was back.

"We need to get back at him somehow."

Finally. Words. It didn't matter where they were coming from. We all knew who the "him" was and we all agreed.

We knew we would never be able to get revenge on Coach Fogden. And if we tried and failed, we knew it would be the last thing we would ever do.

And we also knew this wasn't Matthew's fault. He did what we all wish we could do. Matthew was a hero.

It was Stewart. Stewart was the reason we all had throbbing headaches and could no longer bend our legs. It's all because poor Stewart couldn't practice.

Poor Stewart with his broken nose.

We had to do something.

"Yeah, that was the worst practice of the year. I think I am *literally* dying right now."

"I know. I can't feel my legs. Someone tell me if they are still attached to my body. Please. I'm serious."

"Oh, you're lucky. I can definitely feel my legs, and they hurt like hell."

Bom-bom, bom-bom, bom-bom.

The basketball was still bouncing. It was steady.

"Can someone explain to me why we even had to run today? What did we do?"

"Oh, that's pretty clear. We let Stewart, the O Holy Stewart, get punched in the face. Or something like that."

"Yeah, we didn't somehow stop Matthew from knocking King Stewart back to third grade and Coach Fogden knows we can't win without him this weekend."

"God forbid anything happens to baby Stewy."

"How were we supposed to stop Matthew? That just makes no sense. We knew nothing about it. I wasn't even in school that day."

"Does anything ever make sense with Coach Fogden?"

Bom-bom-bom-bom-bom.

The bouncing was getting faster.

"I can't believe we just had to do all that running because of Stewart. That piece of crap."

Bom-bom-bom, bom-bom-bom, bom-bom-bom.

"Yeah, but what are we going to do to get him back?"

"Let's piss in his locker."

"How about pissing in his lunch one day when he's not looking?"

"Yeah! We could get it in his apple juice or something."

"Who drinks apple juice?"

"How about we just tell on him, fill out one of those stupid bully forms? Dude, he's been taking your math homework every day for the last three years and turning it in as his own."

"Or the time that he pulled your chair out from under you in class and you smacked your face on the desk and then told the teacher you had 'tripped.'"

"Or that he used to throw out Jake's lunch every day because he needed to 'shed a few pounds to get quicker on the court.'"

"Come on. We all know Meadhall wouldn't believe any of those stories and Stewart would find out we told on him. We need something we can really do."

"Yeah. Something embarrassing."

"Isn't the dance coming up?"

"Yeah, this weekend. Why?"

"Do you guys remember what Stewart did to me during the game against Bethel last year . . . ?"

We all did.

The basketball stopped bouncing.

AND THEN CAME GOAT

"But what if something happens?" Elizabeth said to her mother. "If she gets out and gets lost in the house or trapped in something? Cats like to crawl into tiny spaces and not come out."

They had set up a litter box, food, and water, and kept the cat in the bathroom.

Elizabeth's mom wasn't as worried. "Nothing is going to happen. Just don't mess with the animal kingdom and everything will work out."

The cat was named Goat because of the little tuft of hair that grew from just under her chin. Her owners, the Wolfs, were in a fix.

"Please. We know you don't usually take cats, but she'll be fine in the bathroom for a week, just make sure

to change the litter and have her dry food always available," Mr. Wolf begged. Their house had been badly damaged by a tree that had fallen during the hurricane and they needed to move out for a week while repairs to the roof were made.

She never saw herself as a cat person, but when Goat snuggled into Elizabeth's lap and buried her head, Elizabeth melted. The person2person page seemed further away. Goat purred loudly, like medicine.

Elizabeth sometimes wondered how her mother could ever be right about anything, when all she did was watch TV. Elizabeth had never seen her mother read a book, or read anything other than *People* magazine. But she did often seem to be right about animals and their natural order. She was like the dog whisperer, except without her own television show.

No toys, that was one of her animal rules. If there are no toys, no bones, no chewies, then there is nothing for the dogs to fight over. And no cats.

But now there was Goat.

"She keeps getting out," Elizabeth said. She had grown attached to the little Bengal-striped cat.

"Leave her alone. She's a cat. She'll figure it out and so will the dogs. As long as you stay out of it."

When her mother was out at the store, Elizabeth tried picking up the cat and carrying her into the living room. Maybe if the dogs saw Goat in her arms they would know she wasn't a mouse or a squirrel or something to chase and hunt and eat.

But there was something about holding the cat captive that drove the dogs crazy and they lunged at Elizabeth. The cat panicked, twisted and squirmed to be let go. She jumped out of Elizabeth's grasp and darted into hiding, leaving Elizabeth with deep, red, angry-looking scratches all over her arms.

"I told you to leave that cat alone," her mother said at dinner.

Elizabeth pulled her sleeves down quickly.

Not only did Goat ignore Elizabeth's pleas to stay in the bathroom, but she learned to pull open the bathroom door with her paw and she wandered farther and farther out into the house. Then one day, Goat made her way into the living room, where the dogs were resting after dinner and after their evening exercise. Carefully Goat stepped around each one, sniffing their ears and their feet, and sniffing their tails.

It was too late by the time Elizabeth saw what was happening. Denali, the Chinook, was the first to notice the cat tiptoeing around his head. He bolted up.

It didn't take long—one by one the dogs became alert. Willie, the beagle mix, planted his legs and started to bark. Kelly, another mixed breed, began making high-pitched whining sounds, like he could hardly contain himself. The hair on his back pointed straight up at the ceiling.

Goat froze. Her only escape was now blocked by Sadie, the Saint Bernard who had been allowed to return, but at double the going rate, because Elizabeth's mother really needed the money.

Elizabeth felt her heart pounding in her chest. Goat was surrounded. The dogs were in attack stance, growling, ears back, tongues hanging out of their mouths. *Never get in the middle of a dogfight,* her mother had warned her many times. No exceptions. Never.

But she could shout. She could yell and scream and whistle and try to break the dogs' hyper-concentration on Goat. Her wails just seemed to further rile up the dogs. Willie made a sudden move forward toward Goat, barking. Denali responded to the advance by making a second lunge. They had formed a mob in no time. Without a word, without any prior discussion, they ganged up on the cat, each dog taking energy and impetus from the other, to form one single killing machine.

By this time Sadie had gotten her massive body up and was on her feet. She hobbled over and placed herself directly in the middle of all the dogs. Elizabeth held her breath and her tears. Time stood completely still. She watched as Goat hinged her body up onto her back legs, bared her claws, and hissed. She swiped her front paw in the air and caught Sadie right in the face.

That's all it took.

It was all over. Sadie didn't back down, but she didn't attack, either. She leaned her giant head forward and took a sniff of the new "cat" air, then she turned around and hobbled back to her bed, the biggest bed, the one with a lamb's wool comforter, before any of the other dogs could take it. Sadie turned around five or six times, in a counter-clockwise circle, until she felt things were just right, then she plopped her whole body down and went to sleep.

With that, Kelly lost interest and went into the kitchen to sniff for bits of dog food that might have rolled under the counter. Willie got spooked and headed off with his tail tucked between his legs. Denali, too—a little sniff from a safe distance and then he went and laid down. It was over.

Then Goat sat down on her rear end. She lifted her back paw and began calmly grooming herself, licking her foot and rubbing it over her ears and head.

Elizabeth hadn't realized she had been holding her breath the whole time, until she let out all the air in her lungs.

Don't get mad, get even.

If Goat could stand up for herself, Elizabeth could too. And the school dance Friday night would be the perfect place.

TAG, YOU'RE IT

Zoe knew Maggie had put up that Smelly-Girl person2person page. Who else would do that? And who else would get scared and take it down as soon as the power was back on? But it was too late. By tagging so many kids from class, everyone had seen it just before the power went out, and people had added their own little jokes and comments.

There was no doubt Maggie was scared now. And that explained why Maggie wasn't talking about who was going to dress like a freak at the dance tomorrow. That's why she was trying to act all nicey-nice about everybody.

So why had Zoe spent so much of her lunch period holding the table, while Maggie got to go up and get her lunch first? On Italian dunker days that meant only the broken, smooshed ones would be left.

And the school had found out about it. Or at least they heard rumors. Since the page was already down they couldn't really punish anyone, but that's why they were starting this ingenious new lunch table arrangement: Punish everyone.

Instead of letting kids sit wherever they wanted, tables were now organized by homeroom. The idea—presumably—was to break up cliques and prevent students from holding tables for the popular kids and ostracizing those less fortunate, who had to stand with their tray in their hands, pathetically searching for a place to sit. It would force everyone to make new friends.

But it was Zoe who had been pathetic, wasn't it?

The new seating also ensured that kids who had suffered all morning in a classroom filled with students they didn't like and who didn't like them, were offered no reprieve during lunch if their one friend in the whole wide world was in another homeroom.

"You know," Zoe began as soon as Maggie sat down, "someone could have called the Feds and found out who made that Smelly-Girl person2person page. They can do that, you know. They can trace the IP address if they want."

"Well, lucky for whoever did that, it's down now," Maggie answered. Maggie and Zoe shared homeroom. Larissa was three tables away.

Zoe lifted her head. "I guess. Just saying, though." She waited a beat. "But I think they can trace it anyway. You know. I've seen that on *Law and Order*. Nothing is ever really gone from cyberspace. It's in there somewhere."

When a dog on a leash encounters another dog that is unleashed, the unleashed dog will behave aggressively, even if it is a normally unaggressive dog. It's almost as if seeing another of its species, trapped, fallen, weak, brings out the worst.

"And you know the school doesn't have to give students civil legal rights? They can make their own rules and do whatever they want. Like that New Jersey vs. T.L.O. case. Remember when we learned about it in humanities?"

"No, what was that?" Maggie asked.

Zoe didn't even know the girl sitting next to her—which was the point of this new table arrangement—who suddenly joined in the conversation.

"Oh, yeah. I learned about that case. The Supreme Court decided students have no constitutional rights while in school. The state has the right to provide a safe school environment at all costs."

"Yeah, that's it," Zoe told Maggie. "What *she* said."

In the wild, mountain lions have been known to attack their own leader when he appears weak and unable to protect the pride. And circus animals under pressure to perform and suffering from close confinement with other animals—especially ones not of their social status—have been known to attack for no apparent reason whatsoever.

Maggie didn't look so good.

"Are you going to eat those?" Zoe asked, pointing to Maggie's Italian dunkers. "Because if you're not, I'm really hungry."

TROPIC OF CANCER

The first Preston Middle School dance was a big deal. It was always held right before winter break and it was pretty much the first boy-girl event since fourth grade, when everybody still went to the same birthday parties. The parent-teacher organization raised the money and did all the decorations. This year's theme was "The Tropics."

There was some controversy when a few of the parents thought "The Tropics" was in bad taste, considering all the damage done from tropical storm Helen, but in the end it remained. Two large blow-up palm trees flanked the entrance to the cafeteria and leis of brightly colored plastic flowers were wrapped around each banister leading up the stairs. Inside, with the tables folded and pushed against the wall, four rounded stacks of yellow balloons stood in the center of the cafeteria. Tall shoots of green balloons poured from the top, creating the effect of giant pineapples, and the usually bare walls were hung with papier-mâché parrots. It was all very lovely and, well, tropical.

But Elizabeth Moon was a girl with a mission.

Revenge is a dessert best served cold, or something like that.

Speaking of dessert, Maggie was right there, standing at the refreshment table. The table itself was draped with dried grass and more leis. Maggie was dipping into a watermelon-shaped bowl of punch.

It was the perfect time.

"Can I have in on it?"

Elizabeth unlocked her eyes from her target and turned around. "Huh?"

It was Zoe. "I can tell you've got something in mind, something nasty. To be perfectly honest, I don't blame you. If I were you, I'd do worse."

"Worse than what?" Elizabeth couldn't remember the last time Zoe Bellaro talked to her directly, or even indirectly. Oh—yes, she did. At the lunch table just before the storm, Zoe was making fun of what Elizabeth had said in class about her poem. It felt like a year had passed since then.

"Whatever you're planning, I can see it in your eyes. So tell me, what is it?"

Maggie had moved away from the refreshments and they couldn't see where she went. A couple of kids were actually dancing in the center of the room. The DJ music was loud. Lights swirled on the ceiling.

"What are you talking about?" Elizabeth said slowly.

For all Elizabeth knew, Zoe had been part of the Smelly-Girl person2person page too, and just posted a comment to throw people off. And maybe Larissa and probably Justin Benton and who knows who else? And even if Zoe hadn't been part of it, she could have been, in a heartbeat.

It was like one of those scary movies where all of a sudden, all the faces in the room reveal themselves in their true form, scaly green skin and long reptilian tongues, or decomposing flesh and hanging eyeballs, or furry tall ears and fangs.

"Holy moly," Zoe said out loud. "Look at that!"

Zoe's face looked pretty much the same as always. Her mouth was wide open, her eyes smiling. She was pointing to the center of the cafeteria-turned-dance-floor where Stewart Gunderson stood with his pants around his ankles and half his underwear pulled down in back.

"Now that's what I call payback," Zoe said.

What the hell am I supposed to do now?

Swing around and punch this asshole right in the face? Who did it, anyway? Whoever it was is gone. Who had the nerve to pants me? Me?

Zoe is just staring at me, waiting. So are Maggie and Matthew, Ethan. Everyone. Even Coach Fogden and Miss Robinson, standing there, and no one is doing anything.

What I feel like doing is running. Just running away.

But I get it.

I get it. I feel the whole pack of them, waiting. To see what I'm going to do.

What the hell am I supposed to do now?

When Jolie can't do something, when she's tired, or

too sick, or when she has to go into the hospital for oxy-
gen treatments, I watch her face. I know her so well. I
knew her face before I recognized my own. My mom says
only Jolie could comfort me when I was first born. I was
colicky, whatever that is.

She's the one in a wheelchair, but she's my big sister.
When I was really little, like three or four, I tried to imi-
tate the sounds she made. My grandmother was visiting.

"Don't you *ever* make fun of your sister." I thought
she was going to hit me. She never believed me.

Making fun of my sister?

Why I would do that? I would never do that. Jolie was
my "big sister". I just wanted to be like her.

I didn't understand back then, but I do now. People
assume the worst and very rarely does anyone listen. I
stopped trying to convince my grandmother what really
happened a long time ago.

I do know that when my sister's face says hurt and
pain, she makes a joke. She laughs to make *us* feel better.

"Okay. Show's over. No worries, I wasn't dropping my
pants to pee on anyone. Just needed a little air, that's all. "

And that was all.

• • •

Dumping a vat of pig's blood on top of Maggie's head while the whole grade stood watching sounded wonderful but hard to pull off. Getting her to sit down on a chair with special invisible liquid that turned bright yellow and smelled like urine upon contact with fabric also sounded good, but such a concoction might not even exist. Cutting off all of Maggie's hair while she stood at the sink washing her hands might even be dangerous. But armed with her newfound information and a feasible plan, Elizabeth was able to attend the first Preston Middle School sixth-grade dance with an odd, if uncomfortable, confidence.

But then seeing Stewart with his pants down, so scared, and so frozen, and so embarrassed, gave her second thoughts. Elizabeth ran outside and sat down in the hall to get up her courage.

It was funny, right?

Stewart Gunderson had been taken down a notch or ten. Standing there with half his butt exposed, desperately reaching for his jeans and having to bend all the way down to find them, while clutching his underwear in his other hand. Now, that's funny.

No, it was mean.

Whoever did it was just plain mean.

"Are you all right, Elizabeth?" Mrs. Robinson leaned down, with her hands on her knees, and spoke softly.

Elizabeth looked up. Mrs. Robinson was chaperoning with her new husband, Mr. Robinson, although right now she seemed to be alone.

"I'm fine."

"Can I sit with you, then?" Mrs. Robinson asked.

"On the floor?"

But Mrs. Robinson was already beside her, sitting with her legs straight out, probably because she was wearing a skirt.

"I like your shoes," Elizabeth said.

"Thank you, Elizabeth," Mrs. Robinson said. "You know, you are a sweet girl. Very special. And very talented."

Elizabeth looked down at the tile floor, inspecting every smudge and crack, and didn't say anything.

"In fact, I'd love to see you submit your poem to a real poetry anthology. I mean, one that isn't just for our class. A national publication for students."

Elizabeth felt her eyes lift from the ground and settle about midway at the wall in front of her. She could see Mrs. Robinson's hands folded on her lap.

"I can't promise you anything, because this publication doesn't accept all the work they receive, but I know you'll be read. And I know you'll stand out even if they don't choose your poem."

Mrs. Robinson went on. "Or you could just keep writing. And you can show me your work whenever you'd like. You are only thirteen."

"Twelve," Elizabeth said.

"See? You're a good writer, Elizabeth. You have something to say and you say it beautifully."

Elizabeth finally looked up. "But . . ."

"And it's okay to know that." Mrs. Robinson smiled. She pressed her hands to the floor and started to stand.

"Poor Stewart," Elizabeth said.

"Stewart's fine," Mrs. Robinson told her. "Boys will fight and let it go."

"Is the kid who did it going to get in trouble? I mean, did anyone see who did it?"

Mrs. Robinson shrugged. "Let's not worry about that. Come on inside and get something to eat from the luau." She laughed.

"Worry about which?" Elizabeth asked, but Mrs. Robinson was already heading back into the cafeteria.

I hate dances. I hate dresses. I never wear them but my mother said you have to wear a dress to dance. (The truth is, my mother forced me to come when Nadine told her the whole grade would be here, and sometimes you just have to pick your battles. Especially with your mother.) Then Nadine begged me, for once, to be normal, so here I am, at the dance in a dress.

Right now I am expecting to hide in the bathroom, read my book, and wait out the duration of this luau. I really didn't need to see Stewart Gunderson's bare backside—yet another reminder of how stupid middle school is. Anyway, this is a really good book.

No one goes in the last stall, not since it was rumored that there was a peephole from the boys' room, which isn't true, I'm sure. When I hear someone come in, I lift up my feet and wait.

Girls are funny in the bathroom and most of them come in groups and just stand at the sink and talk about their faces and their hair and then walk out again. Then I hear Maggie, and I know it's Maggie because she's humming to herself, and Maggie always hums to herself. It's this song her dad used to sing to her, she once told me,

and I am just about to come out, because I think I should just come out and say hi to Maggie. It's been a long time and maybe we could be sort-of friends again. Let bygones be bygones and all that, right?

Then Elizabeth Moon walks in. And I think, *Uh-oh*.

I guess Elizabeth could just turn around and walk back out when she sees Maggie—and not me, remember, I am hiding in the last stall with my feet up on the seat. But she doesn't. I heard the door open and I heard Elizabeth's voice.

Oh, Maggie. You're in here.

And I hear the door close but nobody's feet are moving.

Oh, Elizabeth. Hi.

Hi.

Now, this is an awkward silence. Everybody thinks that Maggie made that mean Smelly-Girl person2person page with Elizabeth's photo, but of course nobody knows for sure.

I know you did it.

Did what? I hear Maggie answer, and so now I *know* Maggie did it. There's no way she doesn't know what Elizabeth is talking about. Maggie's lying.

Don't bother, Maggie. I was going to get you back tonight but I changed my mind. I'm a better human being than you are.

I really should come out of the stall and get out of here, but for some reason I feel like it's already gone too far. I am already in deeper than I wanted.

Oh, yeah. And how were you going to do that?

I have a love letter you wrote to Mr. Edelman. I was going to read it over the DJ's sound system.

Another beat of silence. I thought I was the only one who knew about Maggie's crush on the school psychologist, Mr. Edelman. She's been in love with him for years, ever since her parents got separated and she used to go talk to him once a week. Did she write him letters? And how would Elizabeth get a hold of one?

No, Elizabeth is bluffing.

But Maggie is too freaked out to think logically. She's the worst poker player. She's not the person you want next to you in battle, let's just put it that way.

You can't do that.

Wait, Maggie really *did* write love letters to Mr. Edelman?

Don't worry. I'm not going to. I won't stoop to your level. You have to live with yourself and what you did.

Okay, Elizabeth, take it easy, I think. *You don't say that to Maggie Carey and get away with it.* But still, I don't move and I don't say a thing. I think my foot is falling asleep.

You don't have any letter, do you, Elizabeth?

Oh, yes I do. It's in my locker.

Elizabeth is a worse poker player.

Good grief.

Look, Elizabeth. I'm really sorry about the person2person thing. I mean, I didn't do it, but it was awful and I bet you feel terrible. We have to stop this kind of thing.

I could hear Maggie's voice change.

Didn't you see what just happened to Stewart? Wasn't that mean? Maggie was really working it now.

I really think we girls need to stick together. This storm really taught me something. I think it's changed all of us, don't you?

I don't know, Maggie.

Wait, I'll text Zoe and Larissa we can all go back out and dance a little bit. Okay? You wanna come?

I hear feet moving. The water turns on and off.

So why don't you go get the letter and give it back to me and we can be friends?

I hear a paper towel being ripped from the metal rack.

Really?

Sure. C'mon. That letter is silly, anyway. How did you get it, by the way?

You'll be mad.

No, of course not. We're going to be in high school in a few years, and we'll look back at this and laugh.

Elizabeth laughs. *Yeah, you're probably right. I'll go get it.*

I hear the bathroom door open. The sounds from the hall and the dance filter in as together, Maggie and Elizabeth's footsteps walk out, and I can't hear what they are saying any more.

I check my cell phone: 9:14. Forty-five minutes to go.

Ethan found himself staring at Maggie in spite of himself. She was wearing a very tight, short black dress that sparkled under the moving pink and orange lights above, so that the dress seemed to shift and undulate even as Maggie stood still at the refreshment table talking to Zoe and Larissa. It was sort of hypnotizing.

When she tossed her head back, laughing at something Zoe had said, her dark hair unwound from around her shoulder where she had been twisting it and spread out along her back.

"What's up, man?" Matthew came up behind him and slapped him on the back.

"Not much."

Matthew followed Ethan's gaze across the dance floor. "Maggie Carey?"

"I know. Screwed up, right?"

"Pretty much," Matthew answered.

Maggie gathered her hair and began twisting it in front of her other shoulder. She was deep in conversation.

"She's the one that made that person2person page, you know," Matthew offered.

Ethan looked away. "I know. I took the profile picture."

Matthew looked surprised. "You did?"

"I didn't really know what it was for. Maggie asked me to get a good close-up photo. You know, I just did it."

"Not cool."

"I know." Ethan felt a slight relief in confessing his guilt, even if in this very safe way, but not much. Maybe it was like his mother used to say, no mistake is too big as long as you learn from it.

Very few kids were dancing. Most of the grade seemed pressed against the wall or sitting at the open tables. There were fans blowing wind over the hula-skirted refreshments table, but that was about all that was moving in the room. Stewart was wisely standing with his basketball teammates, reestablishing his status. Elizabeth Moon walked by, smiling. She was holding something in her hands.

"What's that all about?" Matthew watched as Elizabeth went directly toward Maggie, Zoe, and Larissa.

"No idea, but it doesn't look good."

"Maybe it's a letter bomb and Elizabeth's going to blow that freakin' smirk right off Maggie's face." Matthew put his arm around Ethan. "Sorry, kiddo."

They both watched as Elizabeth handed the letter to Maggie. They watched as Maggie unfolded the letter, glanced at it, and then stuffed it into the tiny black purse that dangled from her wrist. Elizabeth just stood there in some kind of anticipation.

"She's not the girl for you," Matthew said. Both boys watched the scene before them unfold like a silent movie. The three characters—Maggie, Zoe, and Larissa—started to step away from the table. The fourth character, Elizabeth, began to follow. It seemed that she was saying something to them.

Matthew added, "You're the sensitive type."

"I am not," Ethan said.

The three girls in front suddenly stopped, presumably to the sound of the fourth girl's voice, and turned around in unison.

"It's nothing to be ashamed of," Matthew told Ethan. "Just hide it better."

"Is that what you do?"

Across the room Maggie started laughing first, as if she had just heard the funniest thing in the world.

"Nah," Matthew said. "I'm the jester. You know, the court jester? The one who makes everybody laugh but inside he's really laughing at everyone else? Especially the king. I am especially laughing at the king."

"Like that?" Ethan gestured with his chin toward the girls. Zoe and Larissa had joined in to whatever was so hysterical, although apparently Elizabeth didn't find it funny at all. Elizabeth stood with her eyes down and her whole body limp. She didn't move, but she didn't cry.

"No," Matthew said. "Nothing like that. Nothing like that at all."

INSIDE OF A HUMAN

Freida and Elizabeth sat on the curb outside of the
school, both with their knees bent and pressed into their
bodies, huddled close to each other.

"Another reason I hate dresses," Freida said. "My
legs are freezing."

Elizabeth was quiet.

Most of the other kids had gone home, though a few
late rides were still trickling in. There was a police officer
in the street directing traffic, and the chaperones were
checking to make sure everyone was in the right car.

"My mother is always late," Elizabeth said finally.

"Mine never is, so I don't know *what's* going on."

Another car pulled up in the dark.

"Yours?"

"Nope. Yours?"

"Nope."

"Well, the cold is good for you. It makes you tough," Freida said. She jumped up. "C'mon, let's dance around and get warm. That way I can tell my mother I danced at this stupid dance tonight and not be lying." Freida spun once and waved her arms around. "There. Done."

She sat down next to Elizabeth again.

"I'm the furthest thing from tough," Elizabeth said.

"Why, because you didn't take Maggie down? And lower yourself to her level?"

Elizabeth looked at Freida. "How did you . . ."

"Never mind, just trust me. You are better off in the long run. With girls like Maggie it never ends."

They heard the barking before they saw Elizabeth's mom.

"My mom is here?" Elizabeth said out loud. She could see three little wet noses, Winkin, Blinkin, and Nod, trying to suck in as much air as they could from the small crack in the car window.

Freida jumped up again. "Ooo, so cute. Are they yours?"

Elizabeth looked at Freida. "You like dogs?"

"I love animals," Freida said. "You are so lucky. Can I pet them? Oh, wait, here comes my mom, right behind you."

Then, just before she dashed off to her car, Freida turned, smiled, and waved her arm. "Bye, Elizabeth. See you in school."

"Bye."

Elizabeth got into her car, pushing the dogs back as each one tried to jump on her and lick her face.

Her mother looked up into the rearview mirror. "Looks like you had a good time," she said.

"Well, not entirely," Elizabeth answered. "But as long as you don't mess with the animal kingdom, right, Mom?"

"That's right, sweetie."

Elizabeth snapped her seatbelt and let all three dogs press in against her like a warm, breathing blanket, all the way home.

AFTERWORD

The first domesticated dog was born of the wild, the one lupine smart enough to follow behind the band of human nomads who threw their leftovers—scraps of bone and fat and meat—out of their cave. The humans tolerated this wolf, because over time they learned that this wolf had a much keener sense of smell, of hearing, and sight, and, if they paid attention to his movements, he could warn them of approaching predators, changes in the weather, and other potential dangers.

Over time, the wolves got more and more curious, braver, or maybe just more hungry, and the humans got more and more comfortable with their presence. A few thousand years more, and that wolf's children's children's children's children were sleeping at the feet of the humans and eating food meant especially for them.

So *wild humans learned to live with dogs and wild dogs learned to live with humans and both got less wild over time. Only people believed they could understand these domesticated animals, train them, teach them, and force them to live as they wanted, in their new dwellings, not caves but houses, and cars and hotels and boats. They trained the dogs where to sit, where to eat, where—even when—to pee and poop. People believed they understood exactly what these dogs were thinking and feeling, when in reality, the dogs had learned the language of humans far better than the other way around. It was just that the humans had the upper hand—smarter brains and that all-important opposable thumb.*

Humans had more power. Most of the time.

But when you get to be an old dog like me, you stop worrying about power so much. I've had a lifetime of watching the humans. I can tell when they are getting up, going to the kitchen, or going to the bathroom. I know when they are angry and when they are happy. I know when they are about to reach for my leash or press a button on that remote control and sit for hours in front of that horrible light and sound box.

I know when the person at the door makes my humans nervous or confused. I know when they are sick and not behaving the way they usually do. I can't read their minds. I just pay attention. I even know what they think they know about me.

Like I said, I'm an old dog and it's easier this way.

We don't live as long as humans. We don't have the luxury of making as many mistakes, but I think my purpose on this earth is an honorable one. I am of a noble breed, the Saint Bernard, known for our bravery. My ancestors were famous as watchdogs and as alpine rescuers. But me, I mostly sleep these days. I'm tired. My bones are creaky, my eyes are crusty. My hips ache. Humans like us to look a certain way, or rather, many different ways; Saint Bernards, huskies, terriers, dachshunds, Great Danes, beagles, and poodles, but we've had to pay a very high price for that.

Still, I'm not complaining. I've had it better than some.

I can't say I like it very much here, though, with all these other dogs. We are not all of the same intelligence, you know. The one they call Denali is decent enough, but those two little white puffballs are driving me crazy.

But I do like this human girl. She's interesting and she's thoughtful, so she, more than most humans, tries to understand. She knows we are not pack animals, we are not wolves. We do not have an "alpha" male or female, nor do we need one of you to pretend to be one, in order for there to be order.

I am like you. I want to figure out how to fit in and where I belong.

This girl listens—and not just to words, which I've come to learn in my old age mean much less than you humans would like to believe—but she listens to sounds. And she sees the light change.

I hear the sound of the wind, rustling the leaves, as it changes direction outside the glass. Spring is nearing. Fall is ending. The temperature drops. Winter lasts. I watch shadows casting across the room, rising, then lowering, and then disappearing as the day goes on. The girl will come back from the place she goes and comes, the place she calls "school," and most of the time she will be sad. Or agitated. Or nervous.

I know it is the other humans who cause her these feelings.

I don't know how long I will be here with this girl and the older female she is connected to. I can't say for certain how long I've been here already. The shadows have risen and fallen more times than I can hold in my head. But I know I've been here before.

So while I am here I will try to figure it out as best I can. I want to be fed. I want to have a place to sleep. I don't want to be feared, but I don't want to be hurt.

I want to know where I belong.

Just like you.